SoulSearcher

SoulSearcher
Molly Weinfurter

Book cover design by Grace Zimmermann
Book edited by Lacey Verrill

ISBN: 979-8-9903735-2-5 (Paperback)

ISBN: 979-8-9903735-3-2 (Hardcover)

Published by Molly Weinfurter
mollyweinfurterwriting.com

Dedicated to anyone who identifies as asexual and/or aromantic. You matter. ♥

Chapter One
Mila

Soulmates. It's all anyone talks about these days, myself included. But when you feel like one of the only soulmate-less people, you have to find other things to make yourself whole. For me, that's caring for rescue animals. At this specific moment, it's Leo the scruffy mutt.

Leo is the definition of an "Alabama Designer Dog," a term the shelter I work for uses to describe mixed breed dogs that get transported out of overcrowded shelters. He looks like a German Shepherd in the body of a little dog, but his fur is extra fluffy and brindle. One of his ears stands upright while the other one flops. Best of all, he has a big dark spot acting like an eyepatch over his left eye.

Leo is what makes me feel whole today because he's getting adopted! For months, I've trained him at the shelter and gave him lots of love. Now, Leo is finally getting the forever home he deserves. Moments like this are why I do the work that I do.

I hear someone clear their throat behind me. I turn around to see my little sister, Liz, standing in the meeting room doorway with her hands behind her back.

"Liz!" I rush over to hug my sister. But when I pull away, I study her face. "What are you doing here? You never visit me at work."

"Mila, it's here." Her voice is soft, but those three words seem to make time stop.

"Wait, do you mean what I think you mean?"

She smiles and reveals her hands, which are holding a small package with my name on it. "You know, I've never gotten the hype. But you've been talking about it nonstop for years. So, when I saw this outside the apartment, I knew I had to bring it to you right away."

I feel like I'm going to faint, but I try to keep my composure because I can hear voices in the hallway, asking about Leo. They're here! But so is my package. I glance back and forth between the wide-eyed pup and the shimmering parcel that could change my life.

"As badly as I want to open it, I need to send this little guy to his forever home first. Wait right here?"

Liz nods as I lead Leo into the hall. My heart pounds out of my chest for more reasons than one. I approach Janice, a middle-aged woman who's stoked about adopting Leo. She has already met him several times, and I can tell there's a spark between them.

"Hi, Janice!" I call to her. "Leo's so excited to be reunited with you." The woman quickly turns, and her face lights up when she sees her new best friend.

"Leo!" she squeals with delight. "Do you remember me? I'm going to be your new mom."

Leo inches toward her and gives her a brief sniff. When he recognizes the scent, his tail flops back and forth and he scoots closer to her. My heart melts, confirming that I made the right choice selecting this woman to adopt Leo. They're a perfect match.

"If you follow me to the front desk, we can get all the paperwork filled out. Then, he'll be ready to go home with you," I say, motioning for her to join me. The woman and Leo eagerly tag along as I walk toward my coworker, Denise, who works the front desk. "Hi, Denise! Would you mind finalizing Leo's adoption?"

Denise, who was clearly distracted by something on the computer screen, furrows her brows. "Sure. Is everything alright? This is normally your favorite part of the job."

"Yes, everything is great! I'm certain they're a good match and I know you can handle it," I explain. When she still looks uncertain, I lean forward and whisper in her ear. "My SoulSearcher just arrived, and I can't wait to open the package. Please cover for me. This is so important."

Denise gasps. "Oh, say no more! I'll make sure Leo is all set before he walks out that door."

"Great, thank you," I respond. Then, I turn and crouch down to Leo's level. I scratch him behind the ears and give him a kiss on the head. "Goodbye, Leo. Be a good boy for your new mom."

Leo wags his tail as I stand up and pass the leash to his new human. "And thank you so much for adopting him. I can tell you two will have a great life together."

Janice leans forward and hugs me with tears forming in her eyes. I hug her back gently. "Thank you, Mila. You've been so helpful, and it's wonderful to see how much you care about these animals."

When she lets go, I force myself to hold my tears back. I'm often an emotional mess at work. Not because I'm sad the dogs leave, but because I'm overwhelmed with joy when they finally get their happily ever afters.

Once I finish saying my goodbyes, I rush back to the room I left my sister in. It's a cozy space where we have the animals meet with potential adopters. Liz has made herself comfortable on an old couch. When I enter the room, she looks up from her phone and beams.

"Wow, you seem more excited about my SoulSearcher than you were about yours," I laugh.

"Duh. You're the hopeless romantic, not me," she says.

"I'm not sure your boyfriend would be happy to hear that." I'm only teasing, of course. There's no way Sawyer hasn't realized by now that Liz isn't the lovey-dovey type. Although, Sawyer is handsome, so I'll never understand why she isn't more affectionate with him.

As I hold the sparkly package in front of me, I suddenly feel paralyzed. The label says "SoulSearcher Manufacturing." If that wasn't enough to grab someone's attention, it also says "IMPORTANT: Do Not Discard" in bright red.

After taking it all in, I gently rip open the top of the package and pour the contents into my hand. A packet falls out, along with a silver necklace. I hand the papers to Liz, and then I look closer at the jewelry piece. Its pink pendant is a tiny heart-shaped stone that's translucent, but I know it won't stay that way forever.

I clip the chain around my neck and let the pendant fall on my chest. Nothing happens, but it feels like it's supposed to be there. Like it's filling a hole in my heart.

"Well, nothing happened. So, we know I'm not your soulmate," Liz jokes.

"Oh, shut up." But as I grin and look at my sister, some jealousy resurfaces. This pendant is supposed to help me find my soulmate, but my sister, who's two years younger than me, already found hers. She received her pendant way sooner. As much as I tried to feel happy for her, I couldn't stop thinking about how unfair it was. She hadn't even cared about finding a soulmate. She said the only reason she signed up was because she didn't feel like looking for a boyfriend, but if one happened to appear, she wouldn't complain.

I take the pamphlet out of Liz's hands and skim through it.

Congratulations! You have received your SoulSearcher, which means it's time to find your soulmate. Our system has identified a perfect match for you, who has also received their SoulSearcher. Wear this pendant whenever you're in public. It will notify you when you cross paths with your soulmate.

You've received your SoulSearcher as you requested: a necklace with a heart-shaped pendant. Your SoulSearcher is set to light up when you find your match. If you'd prefer a different jewelry style or type of notification, such as music or an alarm, contact SoulSearcher Manufacturing and we can adjust that for you.

I didn't need to read the rest. It was all stuff I'd known since I was a little girl, dreaming about what my soulmate would be like. No one has to sign up for a

SoulSearcher, but come on, who wouldn't? It makes love sound so easy.

Based on information submitted annually, every person in the world who signed up to be in the program is matched with a soulmate once someone highly compatible is within their requested distance. That soulmate could change over time as people change, but supposedly, this necklace will light up when I find the person who's currently right for me.

Since I'm now in possession of my SoulSearcher, that means my perfect match is out there, waiting for me to find them.

Even though you can't sign up for the SoulSearcher program before 18, I've been visualizing my soulmate my whole life. There are a few people who choose to find their partner the old-fashioned way, but I always knew I wanted to take the SoulSearcher route. It just feels so much more romantic. And even though I'm essentially letting fate (or likely a really good algorithm) decide, I've had lots of time to imagine the partner of my dreams.

I picture a tall, blonde guy with beautiful blue eyes and big muscles. He has three dogs and a cat of his own, and his smile is contagious. I imagine he would have a manly name, like Axel.

I glance down at the pendant once more. Suddenly, just wearing it seems like a lot of pressure. "Well, I have the SoulSearcher now, but how am I supposed to find my soulmate? There are billions of people in this world."

"Yeah, but there aren't billions of people in Tampa," Liz points out. "Your odds are better than you think."

"I know, but now that I finally have this necklace, it's so much more intimidating." I pull my gaze away from the pendant and take a deep breath. "And why am I just getting it at 24? You got yours right at 18!"

Liz shrugs. "Mila, calm down. There could be a dozen reasons yours came later."

"Like my soulmate just turned 18? I hope not, that sounds like a baby." Not to mention that Axel, the man I created in my mind, is a few years older than me, not younger.

Liz laughs. "I guess that's one idea. But maybe you didn't have a match that you could logically cross paths with before. Maybe the system didn't think you were as ready as you thought you were. The reason isn't important. What's important is that you can finally do the soulmate searching you've been waiting for. Which is good, because I'm sick of hearing you complain about missing out on love all the time." She nudges me playfully, and I laugh too.

"You're right. I need to start looking right now."

"Don't you still have to work for a few more hours?"

I glance at the clock. "Right."

"Well, I'll see you when you get home," Liz says. "Who knows? Maybe you'll find your soulmate before then."

I know that's unlikely, but as Liz walks away, I can't help but hope I meet my soulmate as soon as possible. I walk out into the lobby, looking at every person I pass. My fellow employees, people looking to adopt dogs, and even the mailman. But no light illuminates from my chest. Not yet, anyway.

Chapter Two
Rory

How do some people walk multiple dogs effortlessly? Here I am, making a fool of myself as I walk to the mailbox with only two dogs: my adorable little mutt, Minnie, and my Chihuahua foster dog, Barney. I've walked the two of them together many times before, but they still like to dart in different directions constantly.

Luckily, walking Minnie alone is a breeze. She's an easygoing Shih Tzu mix of some kind. At least, I think there's Shih Tzu in there. Or maybe Havanese? I've never bothered with a DNA test. She's a 15-pound, brown dog with silky hair.

Minnie isn't the problem on walks though. Barney is.

Despite being eight years old, he has the energy of a puppy. He was surrendered by an irresponsible breeder, so he looks even older than he is. His fur is dull and scraggly, his eyes are a little cloudy, and his breath reeks because of some rotting teeth. Luckily, he has a dental procedure coming up.

But even after missing out on proper vet care his entire life, he craves attention more than anything. I can't believe someone could treat a dog so poorly just for money. It breaks my heart even more when the dog is still loving and trusting despite having every reason not to be.

When Barney walks, he spins in circles around Minnie. He can't comprehend that he's supposed to walk in a straight line. I don't blame him, of course. Many of my former foster dogs also walked like this because they never got the luxury of going for daily walks in the past.

As much as I love having dogs by my side, I always get a little embarrassed when people pass. I probably look insane as I struggle to keep two dog leashes untangled for a walk around the block. On this walk, I need to check my mailbox, but Barney seems to have other plans. He yanks me in the opposite direction while Minnie sits patiently beside me.

Today, like most of my walks, I have my earbuds in with music playing. I listen to music as much as I can because it helps calm me. Even though I've been told I'm the quiet and mysterious type, I love listening to cheesy pop music. I don't care how silly the lyrics are, as long as it makes me feel happy. I've found that wanting to dance or imaging a music video in my head is a great way to make me feel less anxious, at least to an extent.

The calmness I feel listening to music stops when I notice an old man is also grabbing his mail. Everyone's mailboxes at my apartment complex are in the same spot, so it's common to run into someone else. I swear he chuckles when he sees me trying to control my 7-pound foster dog.

My cheeks burn bright red as I scoop Barney up in my arms before he can cause more trouble. I want to turn around and run back home so the man doesn't interact with me, but I haven't checked my mail in a few days. I need to stop putting it off. I tuck my hair behind my ear so my earbud is visible as a way to let the man know that I have no interest in stopping to chat.

Even though people rarely send mail anymore, I try to check the mailbox often. I learned my lesson after my mom sent me a "welcome to your new apartment" gift when I first moved to Tampa, which was almost a year ago now. It had candy bars inside, and since I didn't check the mail for a few days, they became a sticky mess by the time I opened it. Although, to be fair, my mom should've expected that to happen in a Florida mailbox.

But you never know when important mail might show up. Especially since some people, like my mom, still love to send mail for fun. Despite how many times I've explained how to text and video chat with me, she always struggles with it.

As I unlock and open the mailbox, I realize that it's a good thing I did. Besides the obvious spam and unnecessary newspapers, there's a package inside. I set Barney on the ground and grab the contents of the mailbox while holding both leashes tightly. I try to get a good look at the shimmering package, but then, Barney pulls as hard as he can, nearly ripping my arm off. He may be tiny, but somehow, he has the strength of a big dog.

"Okay, okay. Hold on. We can go home," I tell the dogs as I close the mailbox. Then, I remember that the old man is still within earshot. Ugh, I want to disappear. Since I live alone, I have a habit of talking to the dogs a lot. But I often forget that talking to them outside my home is frowned upon by society.

I run back to my apartment with the dogs by my side. I'm amazed I don't drop any mail as I almost trip over Barney's leash on the way. Minnie stops at my door, but Barney keeps walking. He has only been with me for two weeks, so I don't blame him for not knowing where my apartment is. Every door looks the same, after all.

I struggle to unlock the door as Barney pulls to keep walking. Luckily, once the door is open, the Chihuahua shifts his attention toward the apartment and bounds inside.

I'm not going to sugarcoat it, my apartment is tiny. It's a studio, which essentially means it's just one big room. There's a partial wall with built-in shelves that acts as a divider between the "living room" and "bedroom," but it's still a cramped space. I use the shelves to display the various books I've collected over the years, many of which I have yet to read.

Even though I love all dogs, I stick to only fostering small dogs (and sometimes cats) due to my limited space. My home may not be much, but for rescue animals, it's better than being stuck at a shelter.

Once I close the door and free the dogs from their harnesses, I set all my mail on the end table and plop onto the couch beside it. I push aside all the junk mail and focus on the small package. Maybe it's something I ordered and forgot about?

When I get a good look at the label, I feel the color run from my face. It says, "SoulSearcher Manufacturing." Shit.

My fingers hover over the packaging, but as I'm about to open it, my phone rings. I glance down to see my mom's name illuminate the screen. I should be thrilled for a distraction from this haunting package, but my mom is the last person I want to talk to about it. Yet, if I let it ring, she'll just keep calling.

I hold the phone up to my ear. "Hi, Mom. What's up?"

"Does something have to be up for me to call you? I just wanted to hear my beautiful daughter's voice."

"I'm kind of in the middle of something." I can't stop staring at the package with my heart racing.

"Okay, well, do you remember your friend Maria from elementary school?"

"Yep."

"Did you see that she found her soulmate? She finally signed up for the SoulSearcher program this year and found him almost immediately. It was like love at first sight, so they're already planning a wedding. Isn't that wonderful?"

I saw that Maria had posted something about it on social media, but we aren't close anymore. So, I hadn't thought much of it. "I did hear that. Good for her." I hesitate. "Don't you think they're moving a little fast though?"

"No. When you know, you know. Speaking of which, has your SoulSearcher finally arrived? It's about time you found your perfect man too."

I uncomfortably glance down at my mail. The only reason I signed up for this at 18 was because my mom and step-dad made me feel like I had to. And at the time, every person I knew had used a SoulSearcher. Like getting a driver's license, it was just expected. Six years later, I'm still signed up because I'm not brave enough to make a change.

After moving out of Missouri last year to get a fresh start, I realized that SoulSearchers weren't viewed the same everywhere. In Florida, they're still very popular, but I occasionally meet people who date the old-fashioned way or simply don't date at all. That realization almost made me confident enough to cancel my account, but when the annual SoulSearcher questionnaire came around, I chickened out and completed it.

It's silly, but I'm worried my mom will be disappointed if I don't find love like she and my step-dad did. Even though we're hundreds of miles away from each other, I still love her and crave her support. I'm sure she'll love me no matter what, but I hate seeing her sad even temporarily.

I figured my pessimistic answers about love in the questionnaires would be enough to stop me from getting matched with someone, but I guess I was wrong. And since I filled out the most recent one, they have my current address on file.

"Nope. Not yet." I say. "But, Mom, I'm not worried about it. I'm really happy here with Minnie and my fosters."

"I know you are, but trust me, you won't know real happiness until you find love."

When she says stuff like that, it makes me want to barf. Part of me wishes I could tell her to knock it off, but she's my only parent. My dad didn't want anything to do with me, so I've never met him. And my mom met my step-dad when I was in high school, so he never felt like a dad to me.

Now that I live in a different state, I don't have many close friends anymore. If I stopped talking to my mom, who would I have? Minnie, of course. But Minnie won't live forever, and I don't even want to imagine what will happen to me when that day comes. I really do love my mom, but she just doesn't get me sometimes.

"Thanks for calling, Mom. But I have a dog event to get to, so I will talk to you more later," I say finally because I'm not sure how I can even respond. I'm not usually a liar, but I don't want to have this conversation for the hundredth time.

"Okay, I love you. And you better let me know as soon as your SoulSearcher comes in."

"I love you too. Bye."

I hang up the phone and stare intensely at the package again. What am I supposed to do with it? If I mention it to my mom, she'll be so happy, but then she'll also be bugging me for updates daily. I don't want to deal with that.

I take a deep breath as I open the package and dump out what's inside. Sure enough, there's a bracelet, just as I'd requested when I was young and dumb. I'd chosen the simplest design and asked for it to light up because I figured it would draw less attention toward me than a sound might. Even in a big moment like meeting a soulmate, I'd rather not have people looking at me.

As I hold the SoulSearcher bracelet in my hand, I hope that it'll somehow change my mind. That I'll feel excited like I'm supposed to. Minnie and Barney both rush over to sniff the bracelet, and I can't help but smile at their little noses twitching.

But I feel nothing. In fact, seeing it in front of me now, I'm more sure than ever that I don't want a soulmate.

Chapter Three
Mila

As Kiki, my adorable Pit Bull mix, bounds alongside me and Liz during a walk in the park, all my worries disappear. It has been a month since I received my SoulSearcher, and I've worn it 24/7 ever since. Yet, it still hasn't lit up. I just want to fall in love already!

As I slow my pace, I hold the heart pendant in my hand and glance down at it. How can one little necklace make me so happy and so frustrated at the same time?

"Come on, Mila. We're here to get your mind off the soulmate stuff," Liz says.

I roll my eyes. "I know, and I've been trying so hard not to complain about it, but it's eating me up inside. I've been out of the apartment almost every waking hour lately. And nothing! You have no idea how many hot guys I've stared at, hoping my necklace would light up."

Liz smirks. "I've noticed, Mila. You're not subtle about it at all."

"Really?" I drop my necklace and let it fall back against my chest. "I hope I'm not coming across as desperate."

"You're not desperate for wanting to find love," Liz says. "But let's be real, you've only had that necklace for a few weeks, and there are a lot of people in this city. I didn't meet Sawyer until about six months after I got my SoulSearcher."

"That's not reassuring. I don't want to wait months. Or years! Some people wait years."

"And you might not have to. All I'm saying is that it's different for everyone, but I've never heard of someone not finding their soulmate. I'm sure they're looking for you just as much as you're looking for them. As long as you keep spending lots of time out and about, you'll find your match in no time."

I smile. "Thanks, Liz. You almost sound like a hopeless romantic too."

Liz scrunches up her face. "Ew, no. I'm just trying to cheer you up."

I chuckle as Kiki grazes her nose against my leg to check in with me. She sniffs me gently, and then trots ahead again once I make eye contact with her.

I scan the park, which has gotten much more crowded since we arrived. People are walking dogs of all shapes and sizes. If my soulmate is going to be anywhere, it's a place like this. Or a dog rescue event. I assume the person I'm matched with has to adore dogs as much as me, right? I imagine "Axel" is somewhere at this park, petting his own playful dogs. It's hard not to blush just picturing his perfect face.

I shake my head. No, Axel is just a figment of my imagination. There is a real, living guy out there for me to find.

As I'm looking around, my eyes catch a young man about my age running toward a woman sitting on the other side of the park. When the woman sees him, she looks confused at first, but he points to a bracelet on his arm. Then, she looks down at her own bracelet, which seems to be glowing. She beams and quickly gets up to hug him. I can't help but say "awe" at the romantic sight.

I shake my head and turn back to Liz. "How am I supposed to take my mind off my SoulSearcher when people keep matching right in front of me?"

"Worrying about what other people are doing isn't going to make your necklace glow," she responds with a tired voice. She's clearly sick of having these conversations with me, but I can't help it. It's all I think about.

"Why don't they just tell us who our soulmates are instead of making us search?" I ask, mostly to myself. "That would be way less stressful."

Liz laughs. "Whoa, the Mila I know loves the mystery behind the SoulSearcher system. Are you suddenly becoming more cynical? Maybe we're more alike than I thought."

"Well, of course, I love how magical it is. But it's cooler in theory. In romance novels, they stumble across their soulmates so easily, but in real life, it's hard work."

"I think the reason they don't tell you is because they want you to form connections on your own. And because your soulmate may change as you grow. No one can do all the hard work for you."

"Love shouldn't be hard work."

"It shouldn't be hard, but it should be some work. Life isn't a romance novel, Mila."

I frown. "Maybe not, but I want my love story to be as close to a fairy tale as possible. It's not my fault you and Sawyer aren't romantic enough. I mean, come on, you won't even agree to move in with him yet." But then, I soften my expression. "Sorry, I'm not saying I want you to move out! I would miss you so much."

"Mila, I'm only 22. Even if I'd been dating Sawyer for twice as long, I wouldn't be ready. I want to finish school first so I can figure out my future before I make a big decision like that."

"But Sawyer has made it clear that he's ready. I'd kill to have a guy ask me to move in with him."

Liz is quiet for a moment, but then she looks at her watch. She always avoids talking about moving the relationship forward with Sawyer. I don't even dare mention the word "marriage" around her anymore. "Well, speaking of Sawyer, I need to meet him for lunch, so I'll see you when I get home."

She hugs me and rushes back toward the parking lot before I can say more. I decide it's a good time to take a seat at a nearby bench. Kiki seems reluctant to stop walking, but she follows me and lies down beside the bench. She rests her chin on my foot, looking so cute that I have to take a picture of her.

After putting my phone away, I glance around the park at the fellow dog parents. Many of them are middle-aged women, which seems to be the main demographic for crazy dog people.

Then, I notice a girl about my age sitting on a bench near the parking lot. Like me, she's all alone, but a small, scruffy dog rests by her feet. She's reading a book, not paying attention to the world around her.

Suddenly, everything becomes tinted with a pink light. I look around to find the source, but the sun is still shining brightly so none of the streetlights are on. Yet, everything looks illuminated in a different hue.

I look at an older couple on the other side of the park, and at that exact moment, the pink tint disappears. So, I turn back to the young woman reading a book, and it returns. That's when I realize it seems to be coming from beneath me.

When I glance down, I see my SoulSearcher shining so brightly that the pink coloring nearly blinds me.

My heart seems to beat in slow motion. Does that mean Axel is here? I frantically glance around the park, looking for a tall, blonde man with an infectious smile, but as soon as I look at someone who isn't the young woman, my necklace stops shining. I look back at her, and sure enough, the light returns.

I don't understand. Is that girl my soulmate? I shake my head. No, that can't be right. I'm straight. I've only been interested in men before, and I'm pretty sure I indicated that on my SoulSearcher questionnaires. At least, I think I did. Right? I must have.

I look back at the girl once again, and without a doubt, my necklace lights up specifically when I'm looking at her. I have to admit, she's objectively beautiful. She has wavy black hair that's pulled back into a ponytail, and she's dressed in a black tank top with matching leggings.

Her face is buried in her book. Part of me wants her to look at me so I can figure out what's going on. But I also want her to keep reading so I can process this before deciding my next move. If my necklace is lighting up for her, she must be my soulmate, right?

But she's a woman. Is she really my soulmate, or is there a mistake? Have I been attracted to women this whole time without realizing? Am I supposed to go talk to her?

I quickly pull out my phone and type various phrases like "can SoulSearchers get someone's sexuality wrong?" and "why did my SoulSearcher pair me with the wrong sex?" A brief scroll through the search engine confirms that mistakes rarely happen. A lot of people commented saying how they hadn't realized they were bisexual or pansexual until their SoulSearcher matched them with the opposite sex.

Could that be the case for me?

I think back to my childhood, wondering if I've ever been attracted to a girl before. I never even considered my sexuality, but then again, being straight is considered the default by society, so I never had a reason to.

That's when I remember a beautiful redhead that was in my childhood gymnastics class. I had been mesmerized by her even though I barely spoke to her. Since she was a girl, I thought I just wanted to be like her. But if she were a boy, I would've called it a crush. Holy shit. Have I always been bi? Or am I just thinking about the girl from gymnastics as an excuse for why my SoulSearcher is leading me to a woman? How have I never considered all this sooner?

I need to talk to Liz. She always knows what to say when I'm confused. But I also need to talk to my potential soulmate. I won't know if she's a good match unless I talk to her, right? I glance up at her again, but I immediately blush and look down at Kiki. I rarely get nervous, but this is a situation I never could've imagined in my head, so I don't know how to act.

But then, out of the corner of my eye, I see the woman standing up. The little dog beside her perks up as she grips onto the dog's leash and stuffs her book back in her bag. Is she leaving? If she leaves, what happens if I never see her again? I glance down at Kiki, who wags her tail as if to tell me to go for it.

I sigh. This is not at all how I pictured meeting my soulmate would go, but that's the crazy thing about romance stories, right? They always have fun twists and turns. She may not be "Axel," but I should give her a chance.

When I look up, I see she's walking toward the parking lot now. I don't have time to waste, so I jog toward her. Kiki perks up instantly and joins me. As I get closer, I notice that the woman doesn't have any jewelry on. Where is her SoulSearcher?

Before she notices me nearing, I take my SoulSearcher and move it so the pendant is hidden under my dress instead of on top of the fabric. Luckily, the fabric is thick enough to hide the light from shining. Then, I loudly clear my throat once I'm within earshot.

I swear I see her glance at me out of the corner of her eye, but she keeps walking. So, I call to her. "Hi! Sorry to bother you."

She freezes in mid-step and turns toward me skeptically. Her dog, who has shaggy light brown fur, wags her tail, but doesn't seem interested in getting closer to Kiki. I motion for my dog to sit while I assess the situation.

When she doesn't speak, I continue. "I was just wondering, what kind of dog is yours? She's beautiful."

The woman's posture relaxes slightly once she realizes I'm probably not a threat. "Honestly, I'm not sure. A Shih Tzu mix? I found her as a stray a few years ago and I never bothered to get a DNA test done."

"Wow, that's awesome!" I blurt out. My cheeks turn red and I glance back at the little dog. "I mean, my dog's a rescue too."

"Really? Well, your dog is adorable." She smiles slightly. "I adore Pit Bulls. I wish I had more space in my apartment so I could foster some Pitties."

"Hold on, you foster dogs? That's something I've always wanted to do."

I try really hard not to blush as she smiles at me, but it's hard. She's beautiful and cares about animal welfare. That's definitely a good sign. "Yeah, I regularly foster dogs and cats for a local animal rescue," she says.

"That's incredible. I actually work at the Tampa Humane Society, so helping animals is a big part of my life too."

"Oh, I love that place! They do so much for dogs in the community." She glances down at her dog, and then at the ground. "So, why haven't you fostered before? Are you worried you'll get too attached?"

I shake my head. "Actually, no, but I'm sure you hear that a lot when you tell people you foster. For me, I just don't have enough time to dedicate to an extra pet. When I'm not helping animals get adopted at the humane society, I'm a dog trainer on the side. If I fostered too, I doubt I'd be able to have a social life on top of work."

She nods. "I get it. Luckily, I have plenty of free time since I don't have many friends in the city yet. I love the ladies I volunteer with, but they're much older than me, so I don't exactly go out with them often."

"Trust me, I understand that. You're one of the few people my age I've seen at this park."

When there's an awkward break in the conversation, I extend my hand to her. "I'm Mila. And this is Kiki."

She examines my hand for a moment, but then gently shakes it. I get goosebumps as our hands touch.

"I'm Rory," she says. "And this is Minnie."

Rory. My soulmate's name is Rory. I still can't believe she's a woman, but talking to her is making the whole situation seem less crazy.

I don't realize I've been staring into her eyes for too long until she speaks. "I'm sorry if this comes across as rude, but why did you approach me in the first place? Was it really just to ask about my dog?"

My cheeks get hotter. I could say that I just wanted to make a new friend, but lying wouldn't put a relationship off to a good start. So, I reach under the top of my dress and pull out my SoulSearcher necklace so the pendant rests on top of the fabric in plain sight. It's still glowing bright pink. When Rory sees it, the color drains from her face. I can't tell if she's nervous in a good way or a bad way, so I start talking.

"I'm your soulmate. I mean, I didn't realize I was attracted to women, but it lit up when I saw you across the park, so of course, I had to come meet you. I'm still a little unsure about it, but we get along and we're both passionate about animals, so I think the system got it right." I know I need to stop rambling, but I can't. "I've waited my whole life to find my soulmate, and here you are! We should—"

"Please stop talking." Her face is pale as a ghost now, and I think tears are forming in her eyes.

"Oh. I'm so sorry, I should've known this would be a lot for you to take in. I shouldn't have ambushed you like that. I'm so stupid. I swear I don't usually talk this much.

That's a lie, I do talk a lot, but not in rambling sentences like this. This is just all so new to me."

"No, it's not that."

"Then what is it? I'm your soulmate, you can tell me anything." She cringes when I say the word 'soulmate,' which makes my heart sink.

"That's the problem. You're not my soulmate." She tightens her grip on Minnie's leash.

"Huh? What do you mean?"

"I just know you're not, okay? I don't have a soulmate."

"How can you be so sure? Did you not get a SoulSearcher? Are you not attracted to women? We don't have to rush anything if you don't want."

"No, I just know you're not my soulmate. I need you to trust me on this."

"Okay, but I'd like an explanation. Can I at least see your SoulSearcher?"

"It won't prove anything." Her voice shakes. She still can't make eye contact with me.

"Please?"

She sighs. "Fine." She reaches into a small pocket on her bag and pulls out a bracelet. It has a small pendant in the center that's about the size of mine, but it's just shaped like a circle. Her SoulSearcher is so simple that it doesn't tell me anything about her by looking at it. Is that why she's not wearing it? She doesn't like the design?

But when she puts the bracelet on and looks at me, nothing happens. My SoulSearcher continues to shine brightly, but hers doesn't alert her that she's standing in front of the love of her life in any way. There's a hint of surprise in her eyes, but she quickly puts her serious face back on.

"I don't understand. Is your SoulSearcher broken?" I ask. My eyes start to water.

"No, but yours probably is. I'm sorry."

Before I can say another word, she scoops up Minnie in her arms and runs away. I chase after her, but she reaches her car before I can catch up. Of course, even her car is amazing. It's a cute little blue car. I drive a pink car. Our cars would look adorable next to each other.

But thinking about our cars is pointless now because she's driving away. She doesn't look back or even sit in her car for a minute to choose the music before speeding off.

Somehow, I'd managed to find and lose my soulmate in less than an hour.

Chapter Four
Mila

The minute I get home, pull out my laptop and type in search after search. "Rory" gives me nothing, of course. "Rory Tampa," "Rory Dog Rescue," and "Rory and Minnie" get me nowhere either. But I don't know her last name. I don't know anything about her, really. Besides that she's who I'm supposed to be with even though she insists she's not.

Since she didn't tell me what rescue she fosters for, I'm forced to look up every dog rescue I know and see if they have a social media follower named Rory that also happens to be my Rory. No luck. Either this girl has no online presence or I suck at social media stalking.

Oh, shit. Am I stalking her? Is what I'm doing creepy? She clearly didn't want to get to know me, but I *really* want to get to know her. I just want to see a photo of her or send her a quick message. Is that so bad?

Before I can continue arguing with myself in my head, the front door opens. I slam my laptop shut and run to greet my sister. "Liz! Thank god, you're back. I had the craziest day, and I learned so much about myself."

"You just saw me a few hours ago," she says as she takes off her shoes.

"I know. That's why it's so crazy how much has happened. You're going to want to sit down for this."

Liz narrows her eyes, but heads toward the couch. "Okay…"

I run to sit beside her and immediately start speaking faster than I ever have. "I met my soulmate. But you're never going to believe it. She's a woman!" I pause to see Liz's reaction, but surprisingly, she doesn't gasp.

"Really?" she asks. "Are you interested in her or was it a mistake?"

"Well, at first, I was sure it was a mistake. But I really think I could be bisexual. Or pansexual. I'm still not sure I understand the difference between the two." I take a deep breath. "But once I started talking to her, I felt butterflies like I would with a cute guy."

Liz smirks. "Awe, that's so sweet."

"So, you think I could be bi?"

She laughs. "You're the only one who can determine that."

"I know, but you didn't seem surprised. I guess I'm just curious what you think about it. You know me better than anyone."

"I didn't expect you to get matched with a woman, but I don't think it's super surprising."

"Why not?" I lean closer, eagerly awaiting my sister's input.

"I don't know. Being bi is a lot more common than it used to be. And I've seen you staring in awe at female celebrities many times. Even more than you do with male celebrities."

I think about it for a second. She's not wrong, but I'm not sure that it means much. "But straight women can admire a woman's beauty too."

"Of course, but I know you. And it seems like the way you drool over pretty women is the same reaction you have over a hot guy."

"Really?" I ask, but I'm already putting the pieces together. Since being straight is considered the norm, I've never thought too deeply about beautiful women. I'd assumed I was just admiring their beauty as a fellow woman. But I really do feel the same looking at an attractive woman as an attractive man. I can't believe I've never noticed.

Liz reaches out and squeezes my hand. "I'm sure this is a lot to process, so don't feel like you have to label yourself if you're not ready. I'm here for you, no matter what."

I squeeze her hand back before letting go. "Thanks for being so cool about this. I was freaking out about it earlier, but I guess it doesn't feel like a big deal for me. Is that weird? I feel like most people take forever to come out."

"There's no right way to do it. If you're already comfortable with it, then that's great. But it's also okay if you're not."

I smile. I think the biggest reason why I'm not freaking out is because I know the people in my life will be nothing but supportive. I don't think I'll go around telling everyone about it yet, but I know that once I tell my dad and my friends, they'll be just as accepting as Liz. I wish everyone could have a support system like that.

Liz leans back. "I'd love to hear more about your soulmate if you're ready."

"Oh, absolutely. Her name is Rory, and she's gorgeous. And she has a little rescue dog named Minnie. She even fosters animals!" I pause as I gather my thoughts, but I realize that's all I know about her. I consider telling Liz the whole story, but she'll probably try to convince me that my SoulSearcher is broken and needs to be fixed. I don't want that. I've already waited long enough for my soulmate. Why should I wait longer when Rory already seems like a good match? Besides, everything I researched says there are rarely mistakes, so the issue will probably work itself out.

"She sounds like a great match. What else?"

"Um, honestly, I didn't get to talk to her for long. She had a dog volunteer event to get to."

"Oh, that's too bad. When she's not so busy, you should invite her over for a game night. I'd love to meet her."

I shake my head. "No, that's not a good idea." When Liz furrows her brows, I quickly continue. "I mean, that's not a good idea right now. I want to get to know her myself first. Then, you can meet her."

"Okay, that makes sense."

"In fact, I need to go text her some more. Thanks for listening to me." I hug Liz and then run to my room.

My head is spinning, and I don't know what to do next. I just hid something big from my sister, but it seemed like my only option. I'll just have to hope that I cross paths with Rory again so I can get things straightened out. And hopefully win her over.

Chapter Five
Rory

Barney can't contain his excitement as we approach the farmers market's adoption event. Lots of animal organizations and pet-themed businesses have booths set up. Paws & Love, the rescue I volunteer for, has had lots of success at these types of events in the past, so we always sign up to bring adoptable dogs when we can.

Despite bringing Barney to several events since I took him in, he hasn't gotten any interest. I think the main reason is his age. He's not super old by Chihuahua standards, considering that he could live ten years longer if all goes well. But it seems like people are hesitant to adopt any dogs over six years old because they worry they won't get enough time with them. I get it, but those are the years that those dogs need a family the most.

Also, I think him being a Chihuahua contributes to it. Chihuahuas are known for being sassy and mean, but it's not always the case. I hate whenever someone assumes a dog will be aggressive just because of their breed. Sure, Chihuahuas have it much easier than Pit Bulls or Rottweilers, but they still get judged too quickly. I've never seen Barney growl at someone, so he definitely doesn't fall into the Chihuahua stereotype.

When Rhonda, a fellow volunteer, sees me approaching with my overly excited foster dog, she beams and rushes over to me.

"Rory! I'm so glad you could make it," she says. She crouches down and scratches Barney behind the ear, causing him to dramatically tilt his head. Then, the silly pup rolls on his back for belly rubs. "I can't believe this cutie hasn't been adopted yet."

I smile. "Me neither."

A lot of other volunteers don't have time to bring their fosters to every event, but honestly, I'm always looking for ways to fill up my free time. My job keeps me busy, but without having any close friends nearby, I rarely have plans on my days off. While I would like to meet more people, I'm happy that I'm able to help out with the rescue so much. The work is incredibly fulfilling.

Rhonda seems like she's about to make small talk with me, but she redirects her attention when she sees people approaching our table. Being an introvert with anxiety, I'm not great at talking to people I barely know, but these events are an exception. If I can talk about dogs, especially dogs that need homes, I find myself feeling much calmer and more natural in my conversations. So, even though these events are meant to help the dogs, they also help me in a way.

Honestly, I wish I could do something dog-related for a living like my so-called soulmate. I'm a full-time baker at a local bake shop, and for the most part, I love it. But whenever I get roped into helping with the customer service part of it, it's stressful. Dogs are so much more understanding than people.

As Rhonda talks about the rescue with a family, I see a man approaching, so I smile at him. Barney immediately pulls toward him, but I hold the little dog back until I can tell if the man wants a dog climbing on him or not. Luckily, he smiles when he sees Barney's happy little face, so I loosen the lead slightly.

"Hi," I say. "Are you looking to adopt a dog?"

He crouches down and pets Barney. "Yeah, actually. I was wondering if you have any puppies up for adoption."

I'd be lying if I said I wasn't disappointed. In a perfect world, he would've been looking for a spunky, snuggly older dog and immediately fallen in love with Barney. But it's no surprise that most people want puppies. "Yeah, we have a few young ones in the pen over there. And I think Scooter the Lab will be here soon. He's about seven months old."

The man nods and stands up despite Barney wanting more attention. "Great, I'll go meet them. I was hoping to adopt a dog today to surprise my wife for her birthday."

Uh oh. Not another person wanting a 'surprise gift.' Part of me wants to let him go and have Rhonda deal with explaining the rescue's process, but the other part of me is annoyed that people treat adopting a living creature as a casual thing. "Unfortunately, this rescue doesn't adopt out dogs as surprise gifts. We need everyone in your home to meet the dog first to make sure they're a good fit for your family," I explain. "I think all shelters, rescues, and reputable breeders will have a similar rule."

"That's ridiculous. How am I supposed to surprise my wife with her dream gift?"

"Why don't you tell her you're getting her a dog and then pick out the perfect one together so she can be involved?"

He rolls his eyes. "That's not much of a gift then, is it?" My cheeks grow hot as I try to think of the right thing to say. My instinct is to shout "animals aren't gifts!" but I'd never have the guts to do that. And the rescue probably wouldn't be happy with me if I yelled at someone.

The man turns away from me before I can craft the perfect response. "Maybe I'll have better luck with the humane society," he mutters before storming off.

Once he's gone, I breathe a sigh of relief, grateful that he didn't try to argue with me. If he had raised his voice much more, I probably would've cried.

Then, I process what he said. The humane society. As in, the Tampa Humane Society? I glance across the farmers market to see a huge sign for the local shelter. Don't get me wrong, I love that organization and I know they won't let that man walk away with a puppy as a gift. But isn't that the place where Mila said she worked?

There are a lot of people crowded around the humane society's booth, so I can't tell if she's there. I'm not even 100% sure if I would recognize her since I didn't make much eye contact with her.

I shove my worries aside and turn back to Barney. I gently pet him. "Don't worry. We'll find someone who's overjoyed to adopt you. You're such a good boy, and you deserve a forever home."

A few more people come and go while I stand with Barney, but as usual, he's quickly overlooked by the puppies and more desirable breeds. Even so, he's loving all the extra attention. That's still a win.

"Oh my goodness! That Chihuahua is such a cutie," a voice behind me squeals.

I stand up and turn around, prepared to answer some questions about Barney. But when I get a look at the person in front of me, my heart sinks. It's Mila.

She's still wearing her ridiculous SoulSearcher necklace, even though she knows it's broken. The necklace is lit up with a pink hue as she looks at me. I glance around frantically, but fortunately, no one is paying attention to us.

I feel bad for running away from her after our last interaction, I really do. But I didn't know how else to handle it. I've been beating myself up over it all week, but part of me thought I could leave it in the past forever.

"What are you doing here?" I whisper.

"Don't worry, I'm not stalking you. My shelter also has a table at this event and I happened to see you." She doesn't bother keeping her voice down.

"No, I mean why are you over here by me?"

"Because I *need* to talk to you. You're my soulmate."

"I'm not your soulmate and I don't want to talk to you."

"Well, my SoulSearcher begs to differ." Her loud voice causes a fellow volunteer's head to turn. She glances at the glowing necklace, and then at me.

Oh no. I don't talk about my personal life much while volunteering, but now, I'm going to have a hard time avoiding it. I'd much rather only talk about dogs forever.

"Oh my god. Please leave me alone. You're embarrassing me." I whisper.

She flinches slightly and crosses her arms. "There's no need to be rude. I just want an explanation. I think you at least owe me that."

"Fine, I'll do some explaining, but we need to go somewhere private. Give me one second."

Mila smiles and gives me a thumbs up as I scurry over to Rhonda. I tell her I'll be back in a few minutes, and she nods while cradling a puppy in her arms. I rush back to Mila before Rhonda or any of the other volunteers start asking questions.

I scoop Barney up and walk to a bench near the edge of the event with Mila following. I sit down, still holding my foster dog. Mila eagerly sits beside me with her necklace glowing.

Aesthetically, Mila is very attractive. She has blonde hair that falls just below her chin. Her eyes are icy blue with a thick layer of eyeliner around them. She's wearing what I assume is her work attire: shorts and a Tampa Humane Society t-shirt. It's extremely casual compared to the sundress she was wearing at the park.

"So, who is this cutie?" she asks, motioning to Barney. After letting him sniff her hand, she pets him.

"This is my foster dog, Barney." Part of me wants to tell her all about Barney, but I'm not here to chit-chat about dogs. I'm here to clear the air and that's it.

"I love him! He seems so sweet. I wish I could adopt another dog. He seems like he'd love to play with Kiki. She's so gentle with little dogs. They'd be a perfect match. Awe, can you imagine? They'd be a pair of unlikely best friends."

She blabbers on for a while longer, but I'm not listening. I can't stop focusing on her glowing necklace. I worry that everyone is going to see it and think we're in love. I'm not sure why it matters if people think that, but I can't stop worrying about it. "Can you please take off your necklace when you're around me?" I ask. "It's drawing too much attention."

Mila stops petting Barney for a second. "Why does that matter?"

"I just don't like attention, that's all. I'm not outgoing like you."

"Oh, I get it. Just because I'm talkative doesn't mean I always love attention." She keeps smiling as she speaks.

But her necklace is still around her neck, glowing so brightly that it feels blinding. "So, can you please take your necklace off?"

Mila nods and unclasps the necklace. She carefully places it in the front pocket of her purse. Then, she stares right into my eyes. "Okay, are you finally going to stop being mysterious? I'm dying to know why my soulmate insists on avoiding me."

I glance around to make sure no one heard her, and sure enough, there's not a single person within earshot.

"Look, it's nothing personal. I think you're gorgeous and I love that we both value rescuing animals, but you're not my soulmate because I don't want a romantic partner. Not now, not ever."

She furrows her brow. "I don't get it."

"I identify as asexual and aromantic. Do you know what those mean?" As I say it, I realize that I've never discussed it with anyone out loud. It's something that I've been aware of for years, but it never seemed important to bring up until now.

"I've heard those terms, but I don't know how well I'd be able to define them."

I nod, realizing it's time to explain it to the best of my ability. I'm worried my words will come out as a tangled mess or that she won't believe me. But what choice do I have?

I take a deep breath. "Asexual describes people who feel little to no sexual attraction. Aromantic is for people who experience little to no romantic attraction. I don't experience either of those attraction types."

"But I've heard of asexual people being in relationships."

"Yes, there are lots of asexual people in relationships, but that's not relevant. Some aromantic people have lifelong partners too. But for me personally, I don't desire a sexual or romantic relationship, so I've decided that soulmates aren't for me."

Mila is silent for a moment. I swear I can hear the gears turning in her brain as she thinks of what to say. I really hope I explained it right because I don't want to invalidate anyone else on the aro/ace spectrum.

"Wait a minute," she says finally. "Did you know your bracelet wasn't going to light up for me?"

I shake my head. "No, I had no idea what it would do. It surprised me as much as it surprised you. Well, maybe not that much. But I knew I couldn't possibly have a soulmate."

"Why do you have a SoulSearcher if you're certain you want to stay single?" she asks the second I finish my sentence.

I stare at my feet. "All my life, my mom constantly talked about how important they were. I didn't want to disappoint her, so I signed up. I never had the guts to delete my account. Part of me also assumed I'd never get matched with anyone."

"Oh, yeah. Moms can be pushy sometimes, I guess." She frowns and stays silent for a moment. "But you received a SoulSearcher. That means the system matched you with me. They believe that we can be together, so there must be a chance."

"No," I say. The word comes out harsher than I mean it to. "I know myself better than any system ever will. I *can't* experience romantic or sexual attraction. I'm confident about it."

Disappointment is smeared all over her face. I can tell she's trying hard not to cry in front of me. There's an awkward silence between us. Part of me wants to walk away, but I'd feel too bad. I might not be interested in her the way she wants me to be, but she's still a person with feelings. And honestly, she's exactly the kind of friend I've been looking for since I moved here.

"This doesn't have to be a bad thing," I say. "Maybe we could be friends?"

"Just friends?" she sniffles as she says it.

"Yeah, if you're okay with that. I've been living here for about a year, but I still haven't made any genuine friends. And it would be cool to hang out with someone who shares my passion for animals."

Mila is quiet for a moment as she processes it. I've heard that most people don't take "friendzoning" situations well, but she seems surprisingly calm. I'm even more shocked when a grin appears. Maybe she's not as soulmate-obsessed as I thought.

"Yeah, I would love that," she says. "Why don't we exchange numbers so we can figure out a time to hang out?"

My body relaxes. "That sounds great."

I pull my phone out of my purse and open the screen to a new contact. She does the same, and we swap phones.

"I'll text you later," she says after getting her phone back. "I really need to get back to work. But thank you for clearing things up."

"No problem. Thanks for being so understanding. I also need to get back so Barney can get adopted." I set Barney on the ground.

"He's amazing. I'm sure someone will adopt him soon!"

As we walk back to the booths, I see Rhonda waving me over. I say goodbye to Mila, but she pulls me in for a hug before I can walk away. I quickly squirm out of her grasp and rush back to the Paws & Love booth with Barney trotting beside me.

Rhonda rushes over to meet up with me. "Rory, there you are! There's a woman over here who wants to meet Barney. Her Chihuahua recently passed away and she's looking for another small snuggle buddy. I think Barney would be perfect for her."

My face lights up as Rhonda leads me to this mystery woman. When the woman turns around and sees Barney, she beams. Barney runs over to her as if he's known her forever, and right away, I can tell that my sweet little foster pup found his perfect match.

Chapter Six
Mila

I think there's a chance I can get Rory to fall in love with me. I just need to give it time. I know it sounds bad, but we were matched together, so I can't give up completely yet.

Of course, I can't admit that to Rory. I don't want to scare her off. I just need her to get to know me so she can see what an amazing girlfriend I'd be. I've been casually texting her for the past few weeks as friends, and it seems to be going well. She even agreed to a game night at my place.

"Your soulmate is really coming here tonight?" Liz asks as I quickly dust the counters.

"I'm surprised she's a girl. You don't seem like a lesbian." Sawyer, who's seated at the kitchen table beside Liz, chuckles as he speaks. Liz glares at him, but he doesn't notice.

I shake my head, trying to ignore the rude tone in his voice. While Liz is super accepting, Sawyer has been making weird comments ever since he found out. But then again, he has always been a pretty blunt person.

"I'm realizing that gender isn't as important to me as I thought," I remind him.

"Things must be going pretty well if she's ready to meet us," Liz chimes in before Sawyer can say anything else stupid. "Which is surprising to me, because you haven't even talked about her much."

I blush. It has been really hard not to share every detail with my sister, but there's so much about the situation that she doesn't know. Like how Rory's SoulSearcher didn't light up. And how she never wants a partner like that. I feel terrible for lying to Liz, but this seems like something I need to figure out on my own. I will explain everything to her once I'm more sure of the situation myself.

"That's because Rory is pretty shy," I say. "Meeting new people is a lot for her, so please don't bombard her with questions."

"A shy person got matched with someone who never stops talking? I guess opposites do attract," Sawyer says.

"Sawyer, will you stop being such an asshole?" Liz says sharply.

"Whoa, I was joking. Since when did you get so sensitive?"

I glance awkwardly between the two of them. I don't see them fight often, but they're both stubborn, so it gets incredibly uncomfortable when they bicker. I clear my throat. "Anyway, I'd like to avoid talking about any SoulSearcher-related stuff. Even talking about how we met isn't ideal. Rory wants to take things super slow, so we're more friendly than romantic right now."

"Okay, I don't want to overwhelm her," Liz says. "But isn't how you met a pretty big thing? I'd love to hear it from her perspective."

"I think it is, but I know she doesn't want to talk about it yet, so please don't make it weird. I need this to go smoothly. We've only had one date so far, so I don't want to scare her off." That one "date" was just a friendly hangout, but I can't stop this lie now. It feels like the only way to keep the door open for a future romance with Rory. Liz must see the desperation in my eyes, because she nods.

Sawyer doesn't seem as understanding though. I swear I see him roll his eyes. "I'll try my best, Mila," he says, unconvincingly. Sadly, I know that's probably as good as it's going to get from him.

I sweep the floor and try to think happy thoughts. Before now, I had been confident that everything would go exactly as I'd imagined in my head. But even though Liz and Sawyer don't seem too suspicious, I'm worried they'll screw things up somehow. Luckily, my worries fade when I realize that I'll get to see Rory soon.

Liz and Sawyer bring a pile of board games over to the table as I finish cleaning up. They giggle amongst each other and playfully touch each other's arms. I can't seem to look away. It's hard not to feel jealous that my sister found someone so easily while I'm dealing with an insanely confusing situation.

When someone knocks on the door, I snap out of my bleak thoughts and run to the front of the apartment. Kiki bounds beside me with her tail wagging like crazy. Before I open the door, I brush some dust off my floral dress and turn to Liz and Sawyer. "Do I look okay?"

"As always, yes," Liz says with an affectionate eye roll. Sawyer says "no" jokingly at the same exact time.

I take a deep breath and open the door. There, on the other side, is my soulmate. She's wearing a casual navy-colored dress today, which is a new look compared to her usual leggings and tank top. She almost looks like a different person, but in a good way.

She's not wearing her SoulSearcher bracelet, which makes my heart sink a little. But I'm not wearing my necklace either because I thought she would feel more comfortable this way.

"Hi," I say, wishing I could stop myself from blushing. I want to give her a hug so badly. Last time I hugged her, it was obvious she hated it, so I'm done doing that.

"Hey, thanks for inviting me," she says. Minnie waddles into the apartment and sniffs Kiki. Their noses touch, but then, Minnie goes off on her own to explore. "And thanks for inviting Minnie. I'm always more comfortable when she's around."

"Of course! Dogs are always welcome here."

I close the door and guide her to the dining room area, where Liz and Sawyer are already setting up a board game as a way to pretend they weren't eavesdropping. They both put on a big smile when they spot Rory.

"This is Rory," I say. I swear Liz gives me a slight nod as if to say, 'she's cute!' "Rory, this is my sister, Liz, and her partner, Sawyer."

"Nice to meet you," Rory says as she extends her hand to Liz first, and then Sawyer.

"You, too." Liz responds. Then, she gestures to the game board on the table. "We were thinking of playing a trivia game. Is that okay with you, Rory?"

"Yeah, I'm decent at trivia." Rory says softly.

I pull out a chair and motion for Rory to sit. Once she's comfortably seated, I sit in the chair beside her. "Great! Rory and I will be on a team against you and Sawyer."

We take turns selecting our game pieces. Liz and Sawyer scoop up blue and Rory takes black. I would've preferred pink or yellow, but I keep that to myself.

"Okay, first question is for you two. If you get it right, you'll get to move forward," Liz says as she pulls a card from the deck. "Alright, the first question is a nature one. 'What is the largest amphibian species?'"

"The Chinese giant salamander," Rory says before I get a chance to think.

"That's correct," Liz says.

I turn to Rory in amazement. "Wow, great job. Normally, I'm the one who knows all the nature ones."

"Well, animal questions are right up my alley. I'm relying on you for almost everything else."

I giggle. "Didn't you just say you were decent at trivia?"

"Decent in the right categories."

The two of us laugh together, and I notice Liz grinning. "You two are so cute together," she says. Rory's smile fades at the comment, but Liz proceeds with the game before Rory can say something.

The game is rather monotonous. We quiz them, they quiz us. There's very little small talk in between. But then, Sawyer of all people decides to break the ice with Rory and I only a few spaces away from the finish line.

"So, Rory, have you always lived in Tampa?"

Rory smiles. "No, I grew up in Missouri. I moved to Florida about a year ago."

"Why'd you move?" Liz asks.

"I'd never lived anywhere else before and always dreamed of living somewhere warmer. I thought it would be good for me to move somewhere new, at least for a while, to see if I like it. I have an aunt and uncle who live nearby, so that made the transition much easier."

"You lived in Missouri?" I ask, embarrassed that I don't know much about her past. "Is it true that they have a lot of puppy mills there?"

Liz snickers. "Of course that's the first thing you'd ask." I stick my tongue out at her.

Rory nods, ignoring our sibling banter. "Yeah, the breeders are poorly regulated there, unfortunately."

"Wow, that's horrible," I say.

"It sure is. The rescue I volunteered for there took in a lot of puppy mill dogs from facilities that shut down, so I got to help them get comfortable around people and find good homes."

"That must've been so rewarding," I say.

She smiles. "It really was. I'm hoping to do more educating about puppy mills here if I can."

I'm about to keep talking, but I notice Liz holding a card as if she's waiting to ask a question. I smile. "Sorry, you know that's a topic I can't resist talking about."

"Mila, you didn't know where your soulmate is from?" Sawyer blurts out. I want to slap the stupid smirk off his face.

Out of the corner of my eye, I see Rory tense up. "No, we're still getting to know each other," I say quickly. "Some things just haven't come up yet, and that's totally normal."

"And we're not really soulmates, so could you please just call us friends instead?" Rory asks.

Uh oh. I hope my sister will stay quiet, but I can already see her furrowing her brows as the gears turn in her brain.

"Wait, what do you mean you're not really soulmates?" Liz asks. I swear I see Sawyer chuckle.

Rory glances at me for a moment, looking more confused than my sister. "Um, didn't Mila tell you what happened?"

I desperately try to think of something to say that won't make everyone question my morals, but nothing comes to mind. Mostly because I know I've gone about this all wrong, but I don't want to admit it. I did it for the right reasons. I hope they can all understand that.

"I didn't say anything because I wasn't sure if it was something I should tell people," I say quickly. "It didn't seem like my secret to share."

"Oh," Rory says. Judging by the way her perplexed expression fades, I can tell I've said the right thing. "Thank you, I really appreciate that. But from now on, you have my blessing to talk about it with people close to you."

"So, what happened?" Liz asks.

I take a deep breath. "My SoulSearcher lit up for her, but hers didn't light up for me."

Rory nods. "It's because I'm asexual and aromantic. I know I'll never want a relationship like that, so Mila agreed to be friends instead."

Liz's mouth hangs wide open. I expect her to scold me for all the lying, but she doesn't.

"Who doesn't want a romantic relationship?" Sawyer asks. Even though it's an ignorant question, I can't help but agree with him. I can't comprehend why anyone wouldn't want someone to love them on a deeper level.

"Me. I don't." Rory squirms in her chair uncomfortably.

"This is why I didn't want to talk about any of this," I whisper, but Liz glares at me.

"It's okay," Rory says, "Ever since I told you about my sexuality, I've felt a lot more confident about it."

I smile, feeling touched that I'm helping her feel comfortable. But I really wish it was under different circumstances.

"So, why don't we finish up this game? I have a feeling Rory and I are going to kick your butts," I say, hoping to break the ice. Liz and Sawyer seem reluctant to continue after this new information, but Rory nods and resumes playing.

We finish the trivia game, and sure enough, Rory and I are victorious. However, it doesn't feel as good as I thought, considering that there's an uncomfortable energy coming from my sister. Rory must feel it too because she stands up as soon as the game is over.

"I should get going. I have to get up early for work tomorrow," she says, despite only being at my apartment for an hour.

"Okay, let me walk you out."

I lead Rory to the door, and our two dogs follow behind. They had been peacefully napping on the couch.

"Thank you for coming. I had a great time," I say. "And you're a perfect trivia partner."

"You weren't too bad yourself."

Our eyes meet for a few moments, making my heart stop. Every bone in my body is telling me to lean forward and kiss her, but I resist. If I really want to be with her,

I need to be patient and let her come to the decision on her terms. At least, that seems like the right move.

"Well, I'll see you around. Come on, Minnie," she says before clipping on her dog's leash and heading out the door.

As soon as she's out of my sight, my heart aches.

"What the hell are you up to?" Liz says from behind me.

I blush and can't bring myself to face her. "I don't know what you're talking about."

"You purposely didn't tell me that your so-called girlfriend only wants to be friends. She sounds very certain of herself, so you need to stop pursuing her romantically."

I turn around. "Who said I was pursuing her romantically? She's a good friend and I like spending time with her."

"Mila, I know you. You would never give up your dream of romance for a friend you just met. You even cringed as you called her a friend just now. Please tell me the truth so I can help you see the bigger picture."

"The truth? Fine." I cross my arms. "The truth is that girl is my soulmate. My SoulSearcher lit up for her and now I think I'm in love with her. I know she says she doesn't want a relationship like that, but she doesn't know me that well yet. Once we have a chance to bond, I'm sure she'll think differently."

"Mila, do you even hear yourself? You sound insane right now. This girl clearly knows what she wants, and she can't change her sexuality for you." Liz shakes her head. "Besides, you barely know her, so there's no way you're actually in love already."

"Don't tell me that I'm not in love. Only I can determine that. And if she has never had the chance to be romantically involved with someone, how can she be so sure she doesn't want it?"

"The same way a gay person knows they don't like the opposite sex! What has gotten into you? If you care about her, you'll respect her boundaries."

"I am respecting her boundaries. Thinking she'll fall in love with me doesn't mean I'm going to force myself on her. Calm down, Liz."

"I can't calm down. My big sister is wasting her time dreaming of a relationship when she knows it's not meant to be. I'm just trying to talk some sense into you."

"Well, if I recall, not all romances are instant. Didn't it take you like six months before you looked at Sawyer as more than a friend? How do you know Rory isn't like you were?"

"Because I knew I wanted to be romantically involved with someone. Rory knows she doesn't."

"Hold on," Sawyer, who had been sitting at the kitchen table, says. He gets up and puts his hand on Liz's shoulder. "What is she talking about? You didn't love me for the first six months?"

Liz's eyes grow wide. She doesn't look at him. "Well, not in the way I do now. It takes me a while to feel a strong connection with someone. And you know I'm not optimistic when it comes to romance."

"Sorry, I assumed he knew," I whisper.

"You thought I knew that my own soulmate didn't love me?" Sawyer says. "I would've reported my SoulSearcher as faulty if I knew that."

Liz's eyes water, but she forces herself to turn toward Sawyer and look him in the eyes. "Seriously? If you knew it wasn't love at first sight, you wouldn't have stayed with me? You thought I would magically fall in love with you without getting to know you really well?"

"Yeah, isn't that the point of the SoulSearcher?"

"No. It's not! The point is to guide you toward your perfect match, but it's up to the two people to build a meaningful connection."

"Well, apparently you lied to me for six months, so how is that a meaningful connection?"

"I never lied to you. I never even said I loved you before six months. But I love you now, and isn't that what matters?"

Sawyer looks her up and down with narrowed eyes. He shakes his head, and without another word, he walks out the front door and slams it behind him.

Liz cries harder than I've ever seen her. Seriously, she usually has a heart of stone. I don't think she's ever even cried during a movie death. But now, she's bawling like a baby over a relationship I didn't think she cared about that much.

After a few seconds, she wipes her eyes and glares at me. "You know what? Do whatever you want. I don't care."

She storms off in the other direction toward her room. She slams the door behind her. For a second, I wonder if I should go comfort her, but I'm probably the last person she wants to talk to right now. Besides, if she and Sawyer argue, it's usually resolved within an hour or so.

But now that Liz is done bugging me, I can pursue my dream without being tormented. I glance down at Kiki, who wags her tail as if to say she fully supports me. I pull out my phone and call Rory.

"Hello?" She picks up after two rings.

"Hi, Rory. I hope it's not too soon to call. Thanks again for coming tonight."

"No problem. What's up, Mila?"

"Well, the Tampa Humane Society is hosting a charity walk next Sunday, and I was wondering if you wanted to come with me? I don't need to work at it. I'll just be there to walk Kiki and show my support."

She's quiet for a minute. "Yeah, sure. I think I went to one of their charity walks when I first moved here and it was a great time. Minnie might look tiny but she has no problem keeping up during long walks."

"Great, I'll see you then!"

After I hang up, I smile. No matter what Liz says, I know there's a special connection between Rory and me.

Chapter Seven
Rory

I feel sweaty from head to toe as I enter a library meeting room full of a dozen strangers. And it's not because it's over 80 degrees outside. All eyes are on me as I hurry toward the closest empty seat in a circle of chairs. Getting out of my comfort zone when dogs are around is easy, but when it's only people, that's a different story.

"Welcome to the aro/ace support group, everyone!" a woman with bright purple hair announces. If I had to guess, she's probably in her early 30s, but she has an enthusiastic smile that you would expect from someone fresh out of high school. "We're just going to wait a few more minutes as people trickle in, and then we'll get started."

A few people chat amongst themselves while others scroll through their phones to pass the time. I pull out my own phone and check my texts. As usual, there's a new message from Mila. We've been texting non-stop, sharing rescue dog stories and talking about our favorite TV shows. As embarrassing as it is, we both adore teen dramas.

But this text is about something more serious that Mila keeps bringing up: her sister. Apparently, she thinks she caused problems between Liz and Sawyer after the game night. While I don't understand what led to all this tension, I know that Liz has barely spoken to Mila since then, and Sawyer hasn't been back at the apartment since.

Like I have before, I reassure her that it's not her fault and urge her to talk to Liz so things can be less awkward around their apartment.

I'm sure Liz and Mila will get through this, but I'm not confident about Liz and Sawyer. I don't know them well, but from what I saw, they seemed like an odd couple. She seemed laid-back and wanting to take things slow while he seemed very clingy. But I'm trying not to judge since I don't know all the details. I'm obviously not a relationship expert either.

Mila has the opposite reaction though. According to her, Liz and Sawyer will for sure work it out since they're "soulmates." It's weird to think that she still believes in that stuff after her own match didn't work out.

"You're new here, aren't you?" a voice next to me asks.

I look up and see a woman about my age staring at me eagerly. She has dark hair with a blue streak, which is tied back into pigtails. Her eyes are so blue that they could be colored contacts, and her blue eyeshadow matches both her hair and eyes.

I blush and look away so she doesn't think I was staring at her hair or eyes. "Yeah, is it that obvious?"

"No, a lot of aro/ace people are quiet and awkward. No offense," she says with a smile. "I just assumed you were new because I've attended almost every meeting for the past year or so and I've never seen you before."

"Oh. Well, yeah. This is my first time attending. I don't usually do stuff like this, but I figured it was worth a try."

"Well, I hope you enjoy it," she says. "I'm Zaya, by the way."

"Rory."

As if on cue, the purple-haired woman stands up in the center of the circle. "Alright, we're going to get started. For those of you who don't know me, I'm Melody. I'm one of the directors of the LGBTQ+ center here in Tampa, and I'm usually the one who hosts the aro/ace support groups since I'm asexual. I know it's a little cliché, but let's go around the room and introduce ourselves. Name and pronouns, please."

Oh, no. Even though there's no "fun fact about myself" in this introduction, I'm still terrified to speak. Why did I think a support group was a good idea? I've barely talked to anyone about my sexuality, and now I'm about to do it in front of a group of strangers.

One by one, people introduce themselves, starting on the opposite side of the circle. When it gets to me, I take a deep breath. "Hi, I'm Rory. My pronouns are she/her."

"Hi, Rory!" Everyone says in unison. It's a bit intimidating hearing everyone acknowledge me at once.

Then, I remind myself that everyone here is in a similar situation to me. These people won't judge me like the general public because they all understand how I feel to some extent. I'm here to get some answers, and this is the perfect place to do so. I wish that made me feel more comfortable, but I'm still crazy nervous.

"It's great to see you all. Now, does anyone have a certain topic they want to discuss today?" Melody asks.

I start to raise my hand, but I quickly put it down before it even passes the top of my head. I feel like I want to throw up, but I do really want to discuss things. That's why I'm here, right?

"Yes, Rory? Was that a hand?" Melody's smile grows when she says my name. I'm surprised she saw my hand being raised for only a split second.

I glance at everyone in the circle. All eyes are on me. I could lie and say I was just stretching, but I promised myself I would be brave. I take a deep breath. "Um, I was just wondering if it's possible for someone who's aromantic and asexual to be matched with a soulmate through the SoulSearcher program?"

Melody's smile doesn't falter after hearing my weird question. "Well, being asexual and/or aromantic doesn't automatically mean you can't be in a relationship. In fact, some of the people in the group found someone through the SoulSearcher program."

I stare at the ground. "What if they're certain they don't want a relationship?"

"Well, I've never heard of that happening before. Usually, people in that position don't sign up to get a SoulSearcher," she says. "But I suppose it's possible. You certainly don't have to give out personal details if you don't want to, but it would be helpful to know the context."

I blush, unable to make eye contact. "Um, well, that's sort of what I'm going through right now." I know I should say more, but I can't force the words out.

"Feel free to elaborate, if you're comfortable," Melody says. "This is a safe space. None of us will judge you." I look around to see everyone smiling and nodding in agreement. They seem friendly enough, but I'm sure they're already judging me to some extent.

I start talking before I can chicken out. "I signed up for the SoulSearcher program when I was 18 because my mom made me feel like I had to. But I have since learned that I'm asexual and aromantic. I like having friendships with people, but I don't want anything more than that." I pause as I gather my thoughts. "I never got around to deleting my account, and I received a SoulSearcher. I found my so-called soulmate, and her pendant lit up but mine didn't. I'm not sure if this has anything to do with my sexuality, but I thought if anyone would understand, it would be someone here."

The room is silent for a few moments. People shift in their chairs uncomfortably. Immediately, I regret coming. I regret speaking. I thought showing up here and telling my story would give me some clarity, but what if no one understands me? What if I can't even fit in here? Suddenly, I feel like the odd one out in a group of people who are supposed to be just like me.

"Melody, is it alright if I share my thoughts?" Zaya speaks up, breaking the silence. She smiles at me, so I let my body relax slightly. I'm still regretting this though.

Melody nods. "Yes, go ahead Zaya. Just remember to be respectful. This is a tricky situation."

"Of course," Zaya says before turning back to me. "Couldn't you just return your SoulSearcher? You didn't want it in the first place and it sounds faulty, so why not get rid of it?"

Why hadn't I returned it? Every time I ask myself that question, I struggle to find an explanation. It would be the logical approach, but I haven't been in a hurry to do it. "I'm not really sure. I guess I'm still worried I'll disappoint my mom. But I've also befriended the person I matched with, so keeping the bracelet is a memory of how we met, in a weird way."

"Are you worried that this person won't stay friends with you if you get rid of your SoulSearcher?" A random person, whose name I already forgot, asks.

Again, another good question, but for some reason, I hadn't thought about it. "No, not really. But should I be?"

"None of us can really say since we don't know them," Zaya points out. "But make sure you're not leading them on."

"Huh? How could an aromantic person lead someone on?" I ask.

A few people chuckle, but it's an honest question. Zaya frowns. "Well, they wouldn't intentionally. But a lot of people, no matter how understanding they seem, still believe that they can change ace and aro people's minds. So, just keep reminding them that this is nothing more than a friendship and I'm sure it'll be okay."

"I've been upfront about my sexuality and views on romance from the start." I stop to consider everything for a moment.

"Has the other person returned their SoulSearcher?" someone asks.

I twiddle my thumbs as I think. Last time I saw Mila, she wasn't wearing her necklace, but she has never said anything about returning it. "I'm not sure. She hasn't mentioned it, but I'm not sure why she wouldn't. She seems like a hopeless romantic."

"If I had to guess, she's into you and holding out hope that you'll change your mind," Zaya says.

"Really?" Could Zaya be right? I can't imagine Mila doing something so devious, but then again, I've only known her for a few weeks. The thought of losing the first real friend I've made in Tampa hurts, so I don't want to believe it, no matter how likely it is. "I don't think she'd do that. But I'll take your advice and keep being upfront with her."

Zaya opens her mouth to respond, but Melody clears her throat first. "Rory, did you get your questions answered? Because we can move onto a different topic whenever you want."

I'm grateful for Melody's interruption. "You can move on. Thank you."

"I'm sorry, I wasn't trying to come off as rude," Zaya says. "I just know how much a faulty SoulSearcher can hurt someone. That's all."

"Your experience isn't the same as everyone else's," someone points out.

"Wait, can you tell me what you mean?" I ask Zaya. "If you don't mind."

"Of course," Zaya says. She looks at Melody, who nods in approval. "So, I'm asexual but not aromantic. I got my first SoulSearcher a few years ago, and it didn't take me long to find my match. However, we weren't compatible at all. Sex isn't that important to me, but he was crazy about it. He wanted it every day, and I definitely wasn't comfortable with that. Yet, he always talked me into doing it more than I was okay with. I put up with it for a lot longer than I should've, but one day, I realized that my ideal soulmate would never be okay with making me uncomfortable, especially not that often."

She tears up a bit, but then continues anyway. "So, I reported my SoulSearcher as faulty. I knew that if the system is as accurate as everyone claims it is, then there's no way it would've realistically matched me with him. I waited a little while and was eventually matched with someone else. He's a wonderful guy who treats me like a queen. He's not asexual, but he's okay with having sex less if it means I'll be comfortable. If I hadn't turned in my SoulSearcher, I never would've met the love of my life."

"Wow," I say. If I don't encourage Mila to fix her SoulSearcher, will I be holding her back from finding love?

"I mean, that's just my story. It doesn't mean yours is the same," Zaya says. "But like I said, keep being honest with her. Every step of the way. If she's meant to be in your life, she'll stay your friend no matter what happens."

"Thank you."

After that, I'm relieved to sit back and listen to other people talk about their experiences, questions, and concerns. I don't contribute anything else, but it feels good to be able to relate to many of the topics brought up.

At the end of the meeting, Melody stands up. She's still smiling just as brightly as before. "Alright, that's all the time we have for today. Thank you for attending, and I hope you'll all consider returning for our next meeting."

As we file out of the room, I feel a tap on my shoulder. When I turn, Zaya's right beside me.

"Hey, I just wanted to say that I'm sorry if I made you feel uncomfortable," she says.

"I'm always uncomfortable, but you didn't make it any worse," I joke. "Actually, it was really nice to hear from people who can relate. Thank you so much for sharing your story with me. I'm sure it took a lot of guts."

"I could say the same about you. For me, it's not a big deal anymore. I've talked about my love life many times at these meetings."

We walk out of the library and pause before parting ways.

"Listen, it seems like you care a lot about this friend of yours. So, do what you feel is right. And whatever you do, don't change who you are to please her because it will only end up hurting you both," Zaya says.

"Thanks."

She pulls a sticky note and a pen out of her purse and scribbles on it. Then, she hands it to me. "Here's my number. Feel free to call me if you ever need to talk, especially if it's aro/ace related. It's good to have friends who understand your sexuality."

I nod as she waves goodbye and heads to her car. As much anxiety as this meeting caused me, I think it was good for me. It may not have answered all my questions, but now I feel more confident to figure it out as I go.

Chapter Eight
Mila

As I scan the crowd of people and dogs, my heart sinks. The charity walk is going to start in ten minutes, but I still haven't seen Rory. I can't help but wonder if she changed her mind about coming. I let Kiki play with some of the adoptable dogs to pass the time, but it's hard to get Rory out of my head.

"Mila!" When I hear her voice, my stomach fills with butterflies. "Sorry, I'm late."

I turn to see Rory running toward me with Minnie trotting beside her. When Kiki sees the small dog, her ears perk up, but her left one flops over the corner of her eye. I love how her ears don't always stand upright. It adds to her charm. Her tail wags like crazy, although I don't think it has stopped wagging since we arrived.

"It's okay," I tell her. "I'm so glad you could make it."

Rory is wearing her typical outfit with leggings and a tank top. She's holding a box with a transparent top, which reveals rows of cupcakes. Once she's close enough, she holds the container out to me.

"I signed up to bring cupcakes for the bake sale. Do you know where I can put these?"

"Oh, yeah. Follow me," I say, but my eyes only glance at the cupcakes for a second. Since I haven't seen her in person in a week, I'm having a hard time looking away from her beautiful eyes.

I lead Rory to the baked goods table. As we walk, I glance down at Minnie. "Your new foster dog didn't want to tag along?"

"Tyson? No, he was found as a stray, so almost everything makes him nervous."

"That's so sad. In the photos you sent, he looked like a dog who would love to run."

"He probably will one day. But right now, he prefers to hide in his crate as much as he can. Poor guy."

"Awe. If he's ever up to meeting new people, I'd love to see him. He looks like such a sweetie."

When we approach the table that's covered in a variety of sweet treats, Rory hands her box of cupcakes to Denise, who's one of the employees working the event today. Denise's eyes light up. "No way! Are these cupcakes from Sweet Tooth Bake Shop?"

"Yep! I'm one of the bakers there," Rory says.

"Wow, you do an excellent job. I'd recognize these cupcakes anywhere. That place has the best baked goods in town."

"Thank you so much."

"No, thank *you* for making such delicious goodies."

Rory smiles and blushes before turning around. We both step away from the booth so people can gather around to see the treats for sale. I turn to Rory. "I didn't know you worked at Sweet Tooth. I've walked by that place so many times, and it looks adorable."

"Well, I mentioned I was a baker. You never asked where."

"Oh, I'm really sorry. Really, *really* sorry! Here I am, talking about my shelter work and dog training all the time and I didn't even know your job. I've focused so much on your volunteering stuff that I forgot to ask more about your career. Ugh, I'm so stupid."

"Mila, it's okay," Rory says with a chuckle. "I don't love talking about myself, so it's partially on me."

"I just don't want you to think I'm uninterested in your life. Because that's definitely not true."

"It's okay. I believe you. Both of us love talking about dogs, so that's naturally where the conversation ends up." She awkwardly glances around. "So, when is this thing starting?"

I pull my phone out of my pocket and glance at the time. "Any minute now."

People gather near one end of the park, which has a small stage set up. Logan, a manager at the shelter, climbs onto the stage and grabs the microphone stand that's in the stage's center.

He clears his throat before speaking. "Good morning, everyone! My name is Logan. I help run the Tampa Humane Society. I am pleased to see so many people and dogs at our charity event today."

He goes on to talk about all the different booths that are set up, but I already know it all from work discussions, so I let my mind wander. Of course, it wanders to Rory. Before I can stop myself, I'm watching her out of the corner of my eye, wishing she would look at me as lovingly as she has been looking at the dogs around us.

"Alright, that's all I have to say for now. Once you're ready to start the charity walk, you can head to the pink banner over there and follow the arrows. I hope everyone has a great time," Logan concludes.

Rory turns to me and smiles. "Are you ready to walk right away?" she asks.

"You bet!"

We head to the starting point side-by-side. Most of the crowd moves that way too. It's a bit packed as everyone floods through the narrow archway labeled "start here." We let a few larger groups get ahead of us before starting along the trail. After a few minutes, the crowd spreads out as some people speed-walk and others move at a leisurely pace.

"If we're walking too fast for Minnie, just let me know," I say to Rory.

"Oh, don't worry about that. Minnie has a lot more energy than you'd think."

I'm not sure what to say to that, so there's an awkward silence in between us for a few moments. I can't stand silence. Luckily, Rory surprisingly breaks it.

"So, I'm the only friend you invited today? Liz doesn't usually come to these things?"

"Oh, she does sometimes. You know, when she's not busy with schoolwork," I say. "But she's still being kind of distant with me, so I didn't even ask her this time."

"She's still fighting with Sawyer?"

"Yep, as far as I know. And I'm sure you're sick of me talking about it, but I feel terrible. If it weren't for me, they'd still be a happy couple."

"Maybe. But maybe not," Rory says. "You can't put all the blame on yourself. The fact that Sawyer got that mad after one comment proves that there were already problems in the relationship. If they truly care about each other, they'll work through this and become stronger than ever."

I stare at her in awe for a second. Up until this moment, Rory's responses to the Liz and Sawyer situation had been very brief. "That makes a lot of sense. But how do you have good relationship advice if you don't want a relationship of your own?"

"I think it's because I don't get caught up in the feelings and romance of it all. Instead, I can focus more on the logic of relationships. Of course, I know love is important in a relationship, but a lot of times, people in love forget that it's not the only important thing."

I scrunch up my nose. "But when you're in love, it's easier to work things out."

"Sometimes. But sometimes it's just not meant to be."

Ouch. It's hard not to take that personally, but Rory is oblivious to the fact that I'm falling for her. "Well, Liz and Sawyer are soulmates, so they'll be okay."

Rory frowns. "Mila, you know being soulmates doesn't guarantee a happily ever after, right?"

I want to shout, "of course it does," but I'm sure that would freak her out. I hate that she doesn't care about true love the way I do. "Look, Liz and Sawyer fight all the time. That's why I haven't been too worried."

"All the time? That doesn't sound healthy."

"No, not all the time. That came out wrong. Don't worry. I know my sister, and Sawyer's a good fit for her." But as I say it, I can't help but wonder. I'd never been a huge fan of Sawyer, but I'd accepted him without question because he was Liz's match. Liz hadn't talked to me about any relationship problems recently, so I'd just assumed everything was fine. Was I wrong? Am I a bad sister?

Rory nudges me gently as if she can read my mind. "Well, maybe try talking to her again. And don't make her feel bad if she's having doubts about Sawyer. I'd hate for her relationship to come in between the two of you."

I nod, but isn't it normal for romance to get in the way of other relationships? Aren't soulmates supposed to be the most important relationships in our lives? If so, how is Rory content without having one?

"So, anyway," Rory continues, likely sensing my discomfort. "What about your other family, like your parents? Are you close to them?"

Oh, right. This whole conversation started with her simply asking if I ever invited anyone else to stuff like this. Leave it to me to go on a tangent. "I'm close to my dad and he lives just outside the city, so sometimes he'll come to dog events with me. But my mom died when I was in high school, so it's just me, my dad, and Liz."

Rory's eyes widen at the mention of my mom's death. I always feel bad having to bring it up because I know it often makes the conversation darker. But it had to be mentioned at some point. "Mila, I'm so sorry. I had no idea."

"It's okay. Like I said, it was a while ago. And my dad is wonderful. I'm grateful that he was there to support me through those tough times." I study Rory's face, hoping that I haven't made her uncomfortable. "What about your parents? Do they still live in Missouri?"

"Well, I grew up with only one parent. My mom was a single mom. I never met my dad, and as far as I know, he never made an effort to be in my life. My mom still lives in Missouri, so I miss her a lot."

"Oh, wow. That must have been tough."

"Not really. I know we both only have one parent around now, but your situation is far worse, I'm sure. I never felt like I missed out on anything by not having a dad. And since I never knew him, I don't have anyone to miss."

"Do you ever wonder who he is?"

"Not one bit. To me, blood isn't what makes a family. Your real family is the people who show up and care about you."

I smile. "I agree. And your mom sounds wonderful. I'm sure she's proud to have such a kind daughter."

Rory blushes slightly. "Thanks. I wish she wouldn't put so much pressure on me to find love, but other than that, I know she really cares about me." She pauses. "And your parents did a great job raising you too."

Part of me wants to get deeper, but this is a fun charity walk. So, instead, I switch to a more casual conversation. "So, what type of music do you listen to?" For some reason, that makes Rory blush more than the parent conversation did. "Wait, you do like music, right?"

"Of course I do. I love music," she says. "But I'm a little embarrassed by my music taste."

"Why? I don't care what you listen to. Even if it's only music from children's TV shows, I'll still respect it."

That makes her posture relax. "Well, I guess it could be worse. I just like generic pop music. Like, whatever is on the radio is usually enjoyable for me."

I can't help it, but I laugh. "How is that embarrassing? That music is on the radio for a reason. It's popular and catchy. I'm not ashamed to say that's probably what I listen to the most."

"I don't know. A lot of people are music snobs these days. If your music isn't deep or artistic, they'll judge you. But I don't always care about the quality of the music or even the words. As long as it makes me feel something, which most music does, I like it."

Mila nods. "Exactly. So, stop being embarrassed and just listen to whatever you want to listen to. Life is too short to worry about what other people think."

"I wish it was that easy. I worry about what other people think all the time."

"Why would you do that? You're gorgeous and super cool, so I'm sure no one has bad things to say about you." The compliments flow out of my mouth before I can stop them. "And I mean those things as your good friend, of course."

"Thanks, but it doesn't matter. I just get stuck in my head too much, and I don't think any amount of compliments will fix that."

"I don't know, maybe I should keep complimenting you to see."

"Please don't." She laughs.

I shower her with a few more compliments as we keep walking. We're probably at least halfway done with the walk by now, and I'll admit, I'm impressed with how well Minnie is keeping up with Kiki. The two dogs have been walking at a fast pace in front of us the whole time, only occasionally stopping to pee.

I'm not sure what comes over me, but I have the urge to switch the vibes of our conversation. I know Rory hates all the soulmate and true love "nonsense," but it's always going to be important to me.

"Hey, can I ask you something personal? It's okay if you don't want me to."

"Sure, what is it?"

"Why do you carry your SoulSearcher with you if you're so certain you don't want a romantic relationship? Why wouldn't you just return it or report it as faulty?"

She freezes in mid-step and glances at me with wide eyes, but then quickly looks away. Her face turns red, but she continues to walk as she opens her mouth to speak.

"You don't have to answer that if you don't want to," I quickly say. "I've just been curious."

"It's alright. I'm just trying to figure out how to answer that because, honestly, I don't know why." She takes a deep breath. "Curiosity, I guess? I thought maybe I should at least see who my soulmate would be. And I thought maybe the system had evolved to match me with a close friend instead of a partner. Which is what happened, but it still sounds silly when I say it out loud."

"No, it doesn't sound silly at all," I say, even though it makes zero sense to me. "But you're a great person, so I'm sure you could easily find friends on your own. Even without the SoulSearcher, maybe we would've met at a dog event and bonded that way."

"Finding friends isn't as easy as people make it out to be. But yeah, I'm glad the SoulSearcher led you to me."

"I suppose you're right about making friends, but it's different than finding a soulmate. You can have unlimited friends, but most people only have one soulmate."

"Yeah, but there's a difference between having lots of friends and having a few friends that will last a lifetime. I didn't have many close friends growing up, and it has been hard to make friends here since I get nervous talking to new people. That's why I'm happy I met you. I feel like we can have a better connection than most friends do." She glances at the ground quickly. "Sorry if that's cheesy."

"I don't mind cheesy. But when you say a 'better connection,' what does that mean? How is that different than falling in love with your friend?"

"Mila, you know you can be close to someone without being in love with them, right?"

Did I know that? I think back to all my past friends. Liz is the only person I feel really close to besides Rory, but she's my sister. Although, now that I think about it, when I was growing up, I was quick to have crushes on my male friends because we got closer. Was that not really a crush? Did I just assume I liked them because they were boys I knew well?

I glance down at the dogs, who are still going strong and not losing energy. Every once in a while, I see Kiki slow down so Minnie's short legs can keep up.

"If you were curious and didn't want to return the SoulSearcher, then why not wear it?" I ask.

"Huh? Why would I wear it?"

"The only time I saw you wear it was when you proved to me that it didn't work. But don't you ever wonder if it'll turn on at some point if you always wear it?" As the words fall out of my mouth, I realize they could be offensive. "Not in the traditional way, of course. I know you can't have those types of feelings, but wouldn't you be interested to see who it would react to and when?"

Rory scrunches up her face as if to consider this. Then, she reaches into her bag and pulls out her SoulSearcher bracelet. She holds it in the palm of her hand as she walks, staring at it uneasily.

"And if you're not curious, I am," I add. "I think it's odd that you would get one that wouldn't react to anyone. I would be interested to see if it ever does anything while you're wearing it."

She flinches as I talk, but she doesn't look away from the bracelet. Then, she gently slides it over her hand.

Rory admires the bracelet, which just looks like a normal piece of jewelry right now. "Hm, I guess I'll wear it if it makes you happy. After all, I do love the style. I just wish wearing it didn't make everyone think I was out looking for love."

"Like I said before, who cares what other people think?" I ask, even though I know how much she cares. I'd be lying if I said I never cared either. I'm just better at hiding it.

"Now it's my turn to ask you something personal," she says suddenly. I really hope she'll confess secret feelings for me, but I'm quickly proven wrong. "Why haven't you reported your necklace as faulty? Or have you?"

"Oh." For once, I'm speechless. I can't tell her the real reason. But I also don't want to lie. "I haven't reported it yet, but I guess that's just because it reminds me of how we met and became friends. Maybe it's silly, but I don't want to give it up yet because it has such a good memory."

She smiles. "That's kind of how I've felt too. But I was just curious. For me, it doesn't matter if I keep it because I don't want to be matched with someone else. But for you, this could be holding you back from finding love."

She has clearly picked up on how much I want romance in my life. I bite my lip and consider my options. "Well, I don't know. I'll turn it in eventually, but part of me isn't ready yet. Getting matched with you was an emotional roller coaster at first, so I don't want to rush into getting a new soulmate just yet. Which is totally unlike me, but, I don't know. I'm still processing it all."

"That's okay. There's no need to rush into it. You're a great person, so I'm sure it won't be hard for them to match you with someone."

"Yeah." I say, but my mind drifts elsewhere as we continue the walk. I keep glancing at Rory's bracelet out of the corner of my eye, expecting something to happen. I desperately want it to light up when she looks at me, but it doesn't.

And it's finally starting to sink in that it might never.

Chapter Nine
Rory

I scatter some sprinkles on the colorful selection of cupcakes in front of me, giving them a shimmering texture. It's the perfect finishing touch. Even though it's the same job every day, I always try to make each cupcake unique. No two cupcakes have exactly the same amount of frosting or sprinkles because it makes them special. And it sure makes my job less monotonous. Luckily, I'm allowed to listen to music while I work, so my earbuds are always in.

I consider keeping a cupcake from this batch for myself, but before I can go for it, Emilio, one of the cashiers for the day, opens the door just enough for his head to peek through. I jump slightly, hoping he didn't see me dancing along to my music. I quickly take my earbuds out.

"Rory, someone's here to see you," he says.

"Really?" I glance down at myself to see that my apron is a mess of frosting and flour. I sigh. "Who is it?"

"Oops, I didn't get her name. That's my bad. I can go ask her if you want?"

"What does she look like?"

"Um, she has short blonde hair, I think? Oh! She's wearing a purple dress. She's super cute too, maybe you could set me up?" He smirks. By that description, it sounds like Mila. I'm pretty sure Emilio is in high school, so I ignore his creepy request.

I stand on my tiptoes to peek through a high window that has views of the front counter. Sure enough, it's her. I don't want to go out into the lobby looking like a mess, but I don't want to ignore my friend.

I glance down at my wrist and breathe a sigh of relief when I see that my SoulSearcher is there. I'd considered taking it off several times since the charity event, but wearing it made Mila overjoyed in a way I couldn't comprehend. If I take it off, I worry it'll upset her.

"I'll come say hi to her in one second," I tell Emilio.

"Well, now that you know who she is... is she single?" he asks.

I roll my eyes. "This is a pretty unprofessional conversation to be having at work."

His grin immediately disappears as if he just realized he was talking to an older coworker instead of one of his guy friends. "You're right. I'm so sorry." He disappears from the room within seconds.

I toss my dirty apron into the hamper and put on a new one. Then, I throw my hairnet in the trash shortly before exiting the kitchen.

Once I'm outside of the kitchen, I feel like a deer in headlights. The front counter is not my friend. I love being alone with my pastries behind the scenes. Interacting with strangers is not my forte, especially since I get my fill of human interactions through volunteering. But when I see Mila on the other side of the counter, waving to me with the biggest smile in the world, I relax.

I approach Mila, who's standing off to the side while Emilio handles the long line of customers. He glances at Mila out of the corner of his eye, but quickly looks back to a customer when he notices me approaching. Mila leans against the counter as her smile lights up the room.

"Hi, Mila. What are you doing here?" I ask.

"Can't a girl just want some cupcakes?"

"Fair enough. But I'm on the clock, so I can't chat now."

"I'm so sorry to bother you, but it's not just that. I figured this would be a great place to pick out a birthday cake! Would I be able to try some samples by any chance?"

"Wait, is your birthday coming up?"

"Not exactly. My birthday was about two months ago, and Liz's birthday is about two months from now. So, instead of having two parties, we usually plan one big party for both of us that's right in the middle. We haven't picked a date yet, but we could do it any week now."

"Oh, so you and Liz made up?"

She furrows her brow. "Well, not exactly, but I figured talking to her about the party would lighten the mood."

"Maybe, but don't avoid having a tough conversation with her. You can't just distract her with party planning forever," I say. "But yeah, you can have some samples. I'll send a few cupcakes with you, and you can tell me which flavor tastes the best. Then, I'll make it into a cake for the party. Assuming I'm invited, of course." I grin, meaning for it to be a joke, but Mila's eyes widen.

"Of course, you're invited! I'm sorry if I didn't make that clear."

"Mila, don't feel bad, I was just teasing you. Let me go grab you those cupcakes. Does that sound good?"

"Yes, that sounds wonderful. Thank you, Rory."

I smile as I head to the bakery display. A lot of the items have gone fast, so I will need to replenish them soon, but I have a little time to spare. I pull out a small box and fill it with six of our most popular cupcake flavors. Then, I carefully close it and carry it back to the counter.

I place the box in front of Mila and pull out a marker. I jot down the names of the cupcakes on the outside, next to the plastic film where the cupcakes are visible. Then, I slide it to her.

"Wow, these look amazing! How much do I owe you?" she asks.

"These are on the house. But I will expect you to pay for the cake since that'll take a lot more time."

"Rory, I can't accept this. I'm sure you worked hard on these."

"I did, but I'm gifting them to you. Go talk to your sister and make sure everything is okay with her."

Mila nods, and her cheeks turn red again. She glances at my wrist for a second, notices the SoulSearcher, then looks back at me. "Okay, thank you so much, Rory. I'm looking forward to tasting these!"

She runs out the door with the box in her hands. Part of me wishes I could love her the way she wants me to. After all, she would be perfect for me if that's what I was looking for. But that's just not who I am.

"Rory? Did you give those away for free?" I turn to see Emilio staring at me, frowning. "If the boss asks, you better take the blame for it."

"I will, don't worry. I'm about to make some more." I try to sound confident, but I really hope my boss doesn't confront me about it. I know they won't fire me since good bakers are hard to find, but I still get nervous whenever the boss needs to talk to me.

"Good. I don't blame you though. I would've given her free cupcakes too," Emilio says. He stares into the distance longingly, but then he quickly snaps back to reality. "I'm sorry, I shouldn't have said that."

I laugh and head back to the kitchen. But this isn't the first time I've seen someone drooling over Mila. At the dog event, I noticed several people our age checking her out. So, she could easily find a new soulmate if she turned in her SoulSearcher.

But why hasn't she turned it in? Her explanation didn't make much sense when I asked. I shake my head. I'm probably just overthinking it the way I overthink everything.

Chapter Ten
Mila

When I get home, the apartment is silent, but I know Liz is here. I saw her car outside. I take off my shoes and hang up my purse before tiptoeing toward Liz's room with the box of cupcakes in my hands.

I knock on her bedroom door twice and then take a step back. I hear shuffling on the other side, but a minute or two pass without a response. I'm about to knock again when I hear her voice.

"You can come in."

I reach for the doorknob and gently push the door open. I peek inside to see Liz flopped on her bed. The room is dark besides one lamp next to her bed, so I flip the light switch, causing the room to erupt with brightness. She quickly sits up.

"Ugh, why would you do that? You blinded me!"

"Sorry, but I'm leaving it on. It's depressing in here otherwise."

As I walk to her bed, I have to step over piles of clothes. I cringe at the sight of a dirty plate sitting by the nightstand. I hold back the urge to say something about bugs getting in the apartment because now doesn't seem like a good time. She's clearly doing worse than I thought. Rory was right, I should've tried harder to support my sister.

I plop down on the bed next to her and hold out the box. "I brought cupcakes."

"Mila, are you really going to pretend like nothing is going on? I've been moping for a week and a half and it seems like you've barely noticed."

"Oh, I've noticed. Sort of. I've just been busy with more dog training sessions than usual." I glance at the ground, feeling a little guilty. "And I thought you needed space. I wasn't sure if you'd want to talk about it."

She sighs. "You're right. I haven't wanted to talk about it, especially not with you."

"Look, I know I messed up. I should've been more careful with my words. And I should've tried harder to make things right. But you can still talk to me. I'm your sister."

"Because of you, Sawyer doesn't want to see me anymore. He said he thinks my love for him is fake or something like that. Sure, our relationship wasn't perfect, but we had a good thing going and you had to bring your 'soulmate' over and open your big fat mouth."

I flinch as she speaks, but I can't fight back. I've been messing up a lot lately, so she's right to direct her anger at me. But I also know I'm not 100% at fault.

"Liz, I'm sorry. I didn't realize you weren't upfront with Sawyer about your feelings at first. But that's probably because you talk a lot about how honesty is important in relationships."

"Honesty is super important, you're right. But I was much younger when I met him, so I didn't know how to act."

I nod. "Yeah, that makes sense."

She raises her eyebrows. "So, do you understand why I want you to be honest with Rory?"

I blush. "We're not talking about me. We're talking about you. What are you going to do about Sawyer?"

She rolls her eyes. "Honestly, there's nothing I can do. I've tried reaching out so many times, and when I couldn't get a hold of him, I explained everything over text. The ball is in his court now. Which sucks, but I've accepted that it's out of my hands."

I frown and think about how often Sawyer hung around our apartment. It was almost like he was part of the family. "That's it? You're not going to keep fighting?"

Liz shakes her head. She sits up and examines the box of cupcakes in my hands. "You mentioned cupcakes, right?"

I slide the box behind me so it's out of sight. "Stop trying to change the subject. I've always heard that true love is worth fighting for. I really don't think you should give up so easily."

"Oh my god, Mila! I know you're older than me but some of the things you say are so naive. Romance novels and movies aren't real life. If you're really meant to be with someone, you won't have to fight so hard just to have a serious conversation with them." She opens her mouth like she's about to say more, but then she pauses. "So, why am I moping anyway? It's pathetic."

"Huh? What's happening? You're moping because you love him and miss him."

She shakes her head. Then, she leans forward and places her hands on my shoulders. "If Sawyer was ready for a mature relationship, he would be talking to me like an adult instead of avoiding all contact. I deserve better than this, so it's over whether or not he reaches out."

"I don't know if you should be making such a quick judgment right now."

"Honestly, it's not a quick judgment. I've been thinking about it for a while. Sawyer was only okay as a partner. I deserve better than okay. I was used to having him around and I liked that he was committed to me, but he did so many annoying little things over the years that I just ignored because I thought I was supposed to be with him."

"If the relationship was so bad, then why did you never talk to me about it?"

"I always try to be logical, but it's hard to notice flaws when you're in a relationship. I guess I didn't really focus on the issues in the moment." She heaves a sigh. "And come on, you wouldn't have been receptive if I talked to you. You would've just told me to keep fighting for love like you always do."

Is she right? I shake my head. "I think love is important, but I also care about your happiness."

"Then, please, don't question my decision."

"I'm not questioning it. I just want to make sure you've really thought it through since it's a big decision."

"Don't worry, I'm not going to turn in my SoulSearcher just yet, but I'm 99% sure this is what's right for me. I'm an independent woman who has never needed a man in her life. I can't believe Sawyer has made me all soft and emotional." She leans back but holds out her hand. "Now, give me a cupcake. Please."

There's no point in arguing. Liz is stubborn, and I worry that she's right to walk away from love. But this is just a rare case of soulmates not working out. Most of the time they do. Right? I reach back and grab the cupcake box before I can worry about it too much. I hold it out to Liz and open the top so she can admire the flavors better.

"Before you eat any, you should know that these are samples for our combined birthday party cake. You still want to have a party, right?"

"Oh, I almost forgot about that. Of course, we should do it." She examines the top of the cupcake box to look at the flavors written down. Then, she reaches in to pick the most colorful one. She takes a big bite and melts at the flavor. "You have to try this one! It's amazing."

She holds out the colorful cupcake to me, so I take a bite. An incredible explosion of flavor enters my mouth.

Liz takes a bite of each cupcake and then sets them back in the box so I can try them too. Every time I bite into one, I enjoy it even more than the last. I can't believe no one recommended this bake shop to me sooner.

"I can't choose a favorite. They're all incredible," Liz says. "Where did you get these?"

"Rory made them," I say as I avoid eye contact. "She's a baker at Sweet Tooth Bake Shop."

Liz chews slower as she studies my expression. At first, I think she's going to pounce on me with questions, but instead, she leans back and keeps enjoying her cupcake.

"Is she coming to our party then?" she asks.

"Of course, she's my friend. And I already told her about it when I got the cupcakes, so it would be rude not to invite her."

She keeps eating her cupcake as if nothing is going through her brain, but I know she's judging me. I can see it in her eyes.

"Go ahead, say what you're really thinking," I say.

"Mila, I told you what I thought once. I'm not going to keep bothering you about it. If she's really just your friend, then I'm happy for you and I'd love to get to know her better."

I can't help but breathe a sigh of relief.

"Thanks, I really appreciate it," I say. "So, what about Sawyer? Are you inviting him?"

She shakes her head. "Nope. I'm standing by what I said. I know it'll be the first time in a long time without him there, but I'm okay with that."

Her eyes don't water at all as she says it. It's hard for me to imagine giving up on my soulmate so easily, but obviously, there's a good chance I'll have to.

Maybe I've been blindly worshiping the idea of soulmates for far too long.

"This is the perfect one for our cake," Liz says with a mouthful of cupcake. She only has a few crumbs of it left in her hand, but it looks like the colorful one. I smile as I text Rory to let her know.

Chapter Eleven
Mila

I scoop up a handful of streamers and throw them into the shopping cart. Liz stares at the cart for a few moments and then looks back up at me. "Absolutely not."

Instead of listening to her, I grab one more package and throw it in. Liz rolls her eyes, but then she giggles.

"Mila, it doesn't matter how many streamers you put up in the apartment, they're all going to fall down. You might as well save your moncy."

"Then what about balloons? Confetti? I need this party to be beautiful."

"I found the party hats you wanted," Rory says as she returns from the other side of the aisle. She approaches the cart and hands me a package of sparkly rainbow party hats. She glances at the cart and chuckles. "Wow, I think you might need a few more streamers."

"That's what I was thinking!" I ignore her sarcasm and throw another package in.

Liz and Rory both laugh, which makes my heart flutter. I invited Rory along on our party decoration shopping spree because I knew it would be the perfect way to help Rory and Liz get to know each other better.

And hopefully, it will prove to Liz that Rory is really just my friend. Although, I still hope that one day she can be much more. She has continued wearing her SoulSearcher, but I haven't seen it flicker at all.

Liz reaches into the cart and grabs some of the streamer packages. She places them back onto the shelf and speed walks away while pushing the cart. Rory smiles and quickly follows her. My eyes lock onto Rory's ponytail, which swings back and forth as she moves.

I get myself to snap out of it. Then, I run to catch up with them. "Fine, we don't need that many streamers, but trust me, I'll find something even cooler to fill up our cart."

Instead of stopping to wait for me, Liz keeps pushing the cart toward the checkout line with Rory trailing behind. I frown and glance back at the aisles of the party store. There are at least five we haven't explored.

"Liz, where are you going? I'm not done browsing."

"Mila, I have class later today, and we already have more stuff than we can probably afford."

I know she's right, but her attitude doesn't sit right with me. I walk closer to her and gently wrap my hand around her arm. "Liz, can I talk to you alone for a second?"

Liz glances at Rory awkwardly, and I can't help but do the same. Rory looks back and forth between us for a few moments before Liz finally breaks the excruciating silence. "Rory, can you please hold our place in line?"

Rory gives a small nod, so I drag Liz away until I'm certain Rory is out of earshot. I open my mouth to let my complaints be heard, but Liz beats me to it.

"Mila, what's going on with you? You're never this crazy about decorating. We do this party every year, so I think it's time we start making it a little more laid-back."

"Laid-back? This is the one time of the year we see all our friends in one place. It's a big deal to me."

She crosses her arms. "Then why do you rarely hang out with those friends during other times of the year?"

"They're all busy!"

"Rory seems just as busy, but she's been around an awful lot."

"That's because Rory is a better friend than anyone else."

"Are you sure there's not another reason? Are you sure you're not asking her to hang out more than your other friends?"

"Liz, what's going on with you? Yes, I ask her to hang out with me a lot, but that's because I feel closer to her than any of my other friends."

"Look, I love Rory. I'm glad you've convinced me to get to know her better, but every time we hang out, I see you looking at her longingly. At what point will you accept that a friendship is all it'll ever be?"

My face turns red. I know I should deny it, but I can't lie. It's hard not to stare at Rory all the time. She's gorgeous!

"Fine, you're right. Rory is the reason I want this party to be extra special. I want her to know that I'm cool and fun, so this needs to be the party of a lifetime. And not because I'm attracted to her but because she's my friend and I want her to stay my friend."

Liz nods slowly, but I can tell she's unconvinced. "Okay, then."

She walks back toward Rory, but I don't want this conversation to be over. I hate how lately I'm always feeling like the crazy one.

"Hold on, Liz. Are you sure there's not a reason you're avoiding making this party special?"

She pauses in mid step and glances at me. "Huh?"

"Does it have anything to do with Sawyer?"

"Mila, I don't want to talk about Sawyer. That's why I haven't mentioned him again. But you talk about Rory all the time and she's here with us planning this party. So, it felt relevant to ask. You should know better than to bring up my failed relationship randomly like this."

Her eyes look glossy as if tears are about to form, but she quickly snaps out of it. Liz has always been the master of not crying in front of people.

"I'm sorry, you're right. Let's check out and go home," I say.

We both walk back to Rory with our heads held high. The last thing Rory needs to be worrying about is the fact that she's causing a rift between me and my sister. Although, if I'm being honest with myself, Rory isn't the cause. Rory is a good thing in my life and I keep acting like an idiot.

"Is everything okay?" she asks when we join her in line.

We both nod, but don't say anything. In other words, it's a clear sign that everything is not okay. But luckily, Rory takes the hint and doesn't ask any further questions. We start some small talk as we pay for our items and head back out to Liz's car. Rory hops in the back seat and I sit in the passenger seat. I find myself purposely averting my eyes from Rory to make sure Liz isn't judging me.

As we near Rory's apartment to drop her off, she leans forward and taps me on the shoulder. I turn around and my eyes lock with hers. I try not to make a big deal of it, but my heart is racing.

"Mila, would you like to hang out for a little bit? I just realized you've never seen where I live."

Whoa, visiting someone's home is a big step! Well, in a relationship it is, anyway. But Rory and I aren't in a relationship.

"I'd love to," I say. "Liz, will you be okay unloading the party supplies yourself? I can figure out my own ride home."

Liz nods. "Sure, have fun."

My heart pounds as I follow Rory out of the car and to her apartment. Her apartment complex has a few small buildings, each with two floors. Her unit is on the second story with a welcome mat outside that reads, "dogs welcome, people tolerated."

I smile. "I love your welcome mat. I almost bought one just like it."

"Yeah, I saw that you settled for a 'wipe your paws' one instead. I thought it was so cute," she says as she unlocks the door.

When she opens the door, Minnie runs toward us and whimpers happily. Her tail wags so fast that it's a blur. Rory bends down and scratches behind her little dog's ear, causing Minnie to squeal even louder with excitement. Then, Minnie dashes away and sorts through her bin of toys in the corner before settling on a squeaky plush dragon. She runs back over and hands it to Rory. Rory playfully takes the dragon from Minnie before throwing it across the apartment so the pup can chase it.

Now that we're inside with the door closed behind us, I finally get to take in the place. Minnie doesn't run far before bringing back the toy, and I realize it's because there isn't much space to run since Rory's apartment is just one big room and nothing more.

Even though it's small, it's still very Rory. There are several portraits of Minnie hanging on the wall. There's a bulletin board labeled "fosters" with several pet photos pinned to it. I spot Barney's photo in the bottom corner.

In the small kitchen space, there are a few photographs of cupcakes on the wall. They look like the ones at the bake shop. I glance at the shelves on the wall dividing the "bedroom" from the "living room." They're mostly filled with books, movies, and video games. Several dragon sculptures sit on the shelves, acting as bookends. I didn't know Rory liked dragons. I had always been more of a unicorn person myself.

"This place is cozy," I say as we sit down on the couch. "I love the decorations."

"Thanks," she says before scooping up Minnie and cradling her in her arms. "I know it's not much, but it's the perfect amount of space for me and Minnie. And the occasional foster."

I glance around. "Speaking of fosters, where's Tyson? Or did he get adopted already?"

"Oh, he's still here. Like I've mentioned before, he's *very* shy. So, if you peek around the shelves, you'll probably find him hiding in the crate next to my bed. I let him have free range of the apartment, but he rarely leaves there."

I tiptoe over to the bedroom side of the studio, and sure enough, there's a medium-sized dog crate next to Rory's twin bed. Inside that crate, there's a fluffy brown dog sitting as far back as he can. If I had to guess, he's about 30 pounds, but I have no idea what breed he is. Definitely a mutt, but there's nothing wrong with that. I adore rescue mutts.

Tyson looks up at me with sad eyes and tries to scoot further back in his crate. He trembles slightly, so I back away and return to Rory, who's now sitting on the couch with Minnie.

"Don't worry. If he's shivering, it's nothing personal," Rory says. "He's just not used to being around people who treat him kindly. He comes out to eat and drink, and I walk him outside to do his business, but he never wants to go for long walks or interact with strangers. I'm sure he just needs some time."

I nod. "It's amazing that you do this. Maybe I'll try fostering one day. If life ever gets less busy."

Rory smiles. "Yeah, I think you'd be great at it. I love it, and taking in the shy ones is always the most rewarding."

"Well, my goal when I'm old and retired is to foster as many animals as possible."

"That's the dream!"

I try not to let my mind go into romance mode again, but I can't help it. She has the same dream as me. Our future together would be perfect.

For a moment, we sit in silence, but I can see Rory's eyes darting around the room. It's almost as if I can hear the gears turning in her brain. Does she have something important to tell me? Why does she look so nervous?

She clears her throat. "I'm glad you got to finally see where I live. I love spending time with you, but it seems like we usually do stuff related to your life, not mine."

"Oh, I'm sorry—"

"No, don't apologize. It's not like that." She shakes her head. "I just feel like I've been getting to know you really well, but I'm not always the best at letting people get to know me. I want to make sure you get to see bits of my life too."

"I feel like I know you well already, but I'm always happy to learn more." I cringe after I say it. I need to stop coming across as so desperate.

She laughs nervously. "Well, I do have an idea for an event you can join me at." She leans over and picks up a piece of paper that was sitting on the end table. She hands it to me, and right away, my eyes dart to a rainbow in the top corner. The Pride flag.

"I've attended a few meetings of a local aro/ace support group... that's aromantic/asexual," she says. Her voice quivers as she talks. "They said the LGBTQ+ center is hosting a Pride party, and everyone is welcome. It's not until next month, but it's supposed to be a big event with food, games, and everything. I'd love it if you could come."

Once she's done talking, she glances at the ground. I examine the paper closely. It does sound like a good time, but is a Pride party where I belong?

"I'd love to go if you want me to," I say cheerfully. "But are you sure other people won't mind if I'm there?"

She glances up and me and furrows her brows. "Why would they mind?"

"Well, I'm not asexual or aromantic."

"You don't have to be. It's for all LGBTQ+ people, not just aro/ace. Even if you just come as an ally, that's cool too. But I figured it could be a good community to help you feel more confident about your sexuality."

"I'm pretty confident in my sexuality. I care more about the person than their gender."

She nods and smiles. "I'm glad you've figured it out. I only mentioned not feeling confident because, well, you seemed attracted to me when we first met even though it sounds like you've only been attracted to men in the past. I know that can be a lot to process."

She cautiously looks me up and down, as if she's unsure if this is an okay conversation to be having. I smile to let her know I'm not uncomfortable. Of course, I was attracted to her when we met. I still am! But I haven't thought too deeply about my sexuality since those first few days, so it hasn't felt like a big part of who I am.

"I know it's complicated for most people, but it didn't take long for me to be fine with my 'soulmate' being a girl. Since I haven't spent time worrying about my sexuality or being judged for it, I just feel like I don't deserve to be included at Pride events. I've never even dated a woman before, but I'm definitely open to it." Her expression doesn't change as I say that. I'm not sure why I expected it to.

"Trust me, I felt the same way for a while. But they're happy to welcome anyone, as long as they're kind to others." She pets Minnie as she speaks. "Having people to talk to helped me a lot, so I thought maybe it could help you too. And it's something we could experience together. Just think about it."

I smile and fold the paper up, sliding it into my purse. "I don't need time to think about it. Of course I'll go. If it's important to you, it's important to me."

"Thanks, Mila. You're an amazing friend."

Yep, that's me. An amazing friend.

Chapter Twelve
Rory

I glance back and forth between the two necklaces in front of me. Both of them scream "happy birthday, Mila" to me, but something isn't quite right.

One is a silver heart with pink gems on half of it. Mila loves pink and she seems like a hopeless romantic, so the heart suits her. Plus, I can see it going well with the adorable floral dresses she wears. I'm not too happy about the price tag, but this is the first time in a while that I've been close enough with someone to buy a birthday present, so I'm willing to splurge.

The other necklace isn't as luxurious, but it's very Mila. And if I wore jewelry more often, it could suit me as well. It's a purple pawprint. Simple, yet adorable. Plus, the tag says that part of the profits go to an animal shelter. Buying this necklace would make both me and Mila feel great.

A necklace makes sense because Mila used to always wear her SoulSearcher necklace. I thought maybe having a different necklace to wear would be sweet, but what if she takes it the wrong way? What if it makes her sad because she doesn't have a soulmate yet? Or what if she doesn't need a new necklace because she'll have a new SoulSearcher soon? Ugh. Why is choosing a gift so hard?

The longer I look at the necklaces, the more it feels wrong. Jewelry is such a generic gift. It's what you get for a mom on Mother's Day when you're young and not sure what her hobbies are. It's what you get for a girlfriend on a first Valentine's Day because you're still getting to know her.

Sure, I haven't known Mila for long, but I consider her a good friend. She deserves something more personal than jewelry. Right? Or will it seem like I'm trying too hard to make friends if I get something super specific?

"Hey, Rory! Is that you?"

I turn around to see Zaya, my friend from the support group, approaching me. Her fingers are interlocked with a man who I assume is her partner. Her smile grows when she realizes that it is me.

I open my mouth to speak, but she turns to her partner first. "Blake, this is Rory from my support group." He waves to me before Zaya continues. "You can go ahead and keep shopping around the mall without me while I catch up with her."

"Sounds good," he says. "Nice to meet you, Rory."

He kisses Zaya on the cheek before speed walking out of the shop. I'm left to awkwardly stand there with a woman I only sort of know. We've texted a few times outside of the support group, but that's it.

"You don't have to take time out of your day to talk to me," I say. "I'm just doing some quick shopping. And I'm sure I'll see you at the next support group."

She smirks and puts her hands on her hips. "Is that your way of telling me that you don't like talking to me?"

"No! Not at all. I'm just not great at making new friends." I pause for a moment. "Wow, that sounded really lame coming from a grown woman's mouth."

Zaya laughs. "Girl, don't worry about it. You're never too old to stop learning. And I'm glad you consider me a new friend. How have you been?"

I glance back at the necklaces. "Good, I guess. But I could actually use some advice. I think."

"You think? What kind of advice?"

"Do you remember that girl I talked about at the first meeting?"

She nods, but her grin falters for a second.

I take a deep breath and hold out the necklaces to her. "Well, I'm attending her birthday party soon, and I was wondering, do either of these seem like a good gift for someone who's a close friend?"

It takes her a moment to process what I just said, but then she carefully looks at each necklace. Her perplexed frown doesn't make me feel any better. Then, she glances at the SoulSearcher bracelet on my wrist for a split second but doesn't say anything about it.

"She loves dogs and the color pink if that helps," I add.

Zaya takes her eyes off the necklaces and stares right into my eyes. "I don't know the whole situation, but unless this girl is obsessed with necklaces, I don't think jewelry is the right move. It's kind of giving romance vibes."

"That's what I was worried about," I say. I carefully put the necklaces back on the shelf, but it doesn't help me relax. I'm standing in the middle of a jewelry store with no idea what to get for my friend. Besides the fact that I don't want to buy jewelry anymore. "Do you happen to have any suggestions?"

"Well, what do you want to convey with this gift? Maybe something generic would work if she's someone you just casually know, but if she's becoming like your best friend, I think you should get something to show how much you value the friendship."

"I would prefer to get her something heartfelt. But considering how we met, I don't want her to get the wrong idea and think it's a romantic gesture."

"Doesn't she understand your sexuality by now?"

"As much as anyone who isn't ace or aro can."

"Then I don't see the harm in choosing a meaningful gift, as long as there are no hearts or red roses involved. You mentioned she loves dogs, so maybe lean into that instead of the color pink."

I nod. Dogs are an easy topic for me. I've bought lots of dog stuff for myself, and Mila seems to have a similar taste in dog-related decor. But anyone could buy a generic dog gift. What would be special to Mila? She loves dogs on a deeper level than the average person, so not just any dog gift will do.

After a few moments, a smile appears on my face without me controlling it. "Oh, I think I have an idea. But I need to go home and do some research first."

"Is that your way of ending our conversation without hurting my feelings?" Zaya says. When she sees me get flustered, she laughs and affectionately taps my shoulder. "I'm only teasing you. Sorry, I know I can be a bit much, but it's been great talking to you. I hope to see you at the next meeting. Oh, and hopefully, at the Pride party too!"

"Of course, I'd love to come and maybe even help set up. Mila, my friend, might come to the party too."

Her eyes widen. "Sounds great. I can't wait to meet her."

Then, we go our separate ways. The gift I need isn't something I can find at any stores in the mall.

Chapter Thirteen
Mila

My face lights up as soon as I see my dad approaching the table Liz and I are sitting at. He has a big smile across his face as always. We both get up to give him a hug.

Even though he lives in the area, it has been over a month since we've seen him last. In fact, I know it was before the whole soulmate thing happened for me. Life has just been so busy.

"I'm so happy to see you two," he says once we've all sat down. "Our lunch dates haven't been very frequent lately and I know that's on me. This new job is working me so hard, but I love it."

"Oh, no, it's not your fault. We've been so busy too. I'm sorry I haven't called as much lately," I say.

"Your big birthday party of the year is tomorrow, right?" he asks. "I'm sure party planning is keeping you extra busy."

"Yeah, we're really excited," Liz replies. She pauses for a second as if to figure out what she should say next. "And I know I mentioned this over the phone briefly, but I just wanted to let you know that things are for sure over with me and Sawyer. I hope you can understand."

My eyes grow wide because I genuinely have no idea how he feels about Liz and Sawyer. Our mom had always been obsessed with soulmates like me, but my dad rarely shares his opinion on the topic.

I feel a wave of relief for Liz as our dad relaxes his shoulders and smiles. "Lizzie, as long as you're happy with your decision, I'm happy."

Liz studies his face for a moment and smirks. "You didn't like Sawyer, did you?"

He laughs almost instantly, but to my surprise, he nods. "I'm so bad at hiding how I feel. You're right, I've never been a huge fan of his, but I kept it to myself because you said he made you happy. But looking back, I felt like he was always trying to dull your sparkle a little bit and make you someone you're not."

For a second, Liz's smile fades as she processes that information. Honesty was always a weird thing for our dad. He would either leave out way too many details or be extremely blunt. There was never an in between.

Luckily, Liz giggles in response. "Yeah, you're right. It's so easy to see that now, but while we were together, I didn't think about it much."

He nods. "That seems to happen a lot, especially in this world where soulmates are assigned to you. I got lucky with your mom, but I see so many people ignoring bad behaviors in their partners just because that's their 'soulmate.'"

Liz glances at me out of the corner of her eye, but I pretend I don't notice. I know why she's looking at me. I've always believed that soulmates are perfect for each other without question. But after meeting Rory and seeing things fall apart with Liz and Sawyer, I don't know what to think anymore.

"Anyway, Mila, how's your soulmate? Last time we talked on the phone, you had recently matched with someone, but you didn't give me many details," my dad says. "The silence is so unlike you. I hope everything is okay."

I blush. I know I've texted him since then, but I guess I hadn't taken a moment to give him an important update on my life. But how was I supposed to explain it all?

"Okay, Liz also called me about it after it happened, and she accidentally let it slip that your soulmate is a girl," he adds. I glare at Liz for a moment, and she mouths 'sorry.' "So, please don't feel nervous about coming out to me. I don't care if you're gay, bi, whatever. I love you no matter what."

His words make me feel warm and fuzzy inside. I wish I could talk about Rory as if she's my girlfriend. But she isn't. And if I lie about it, I know Liz will call me out on my bullshit.

"Actually, Dad, I don't have a soulmate right now. I matched with a wonderful woman named Rory, but her SoulSearcher didn't react to mine and she doesn't want a relationship with anyone. But she has become a good friend, so I'm actually kind of glad things happened the way they did." As I speak, I find myself really starting to believe my words. I still feel terrible for lying to Liz when this all started, so I don't want to lie to my dad too. "But, yeah, I'm not straight. I don't know what the label is, probably bi or pan, but I'm open to dating both men and women. I'm happy you're okay with that."

My dad keeps smiling, and he reaches across the table to hold my hand. "Wow, that's a lot to take in, but I'm happy you told me. And I'm sorry that your first soulmate situation didn't work out, but don't forget, a good friend can be just as valuable as a romantic partner."

I squeeze his hand gently. "Thanks, but I'm sure Mom wouldn't have agreed with you."

For a second, I worry that I shouldn't have said that. It has been years since my mom died, but it still randomly hurts sometimes for me. I'm sure it's the same for Liz and my dad.

"You're right, Mila," he says after a few quiet moments. "Your mom believed in the SoulSearchers a little too much. I sometimes wish she wouldn't have drilled into your head how important they are, but at the same time, I admired her optimism. Her SoulSearcher led her to me, which obviously worked out well. I think she liked to assume that everyone's story worked out perfectly too."

"I didn't mean anything bad by saying that. I love how much Mom respected SoulSearchers. It's the reason I care about them so much," I say.

"I'm glad you love the system like she did, but I want to make sure it doesn't take over your life."

"What do you mean?"

"I mean, I worry that you'll end up getting matched with someone that isn't a good fit and you'll be hesitant to leave because you believe in SoulSearchers so heavily. And I worry you won't value your other relationships, such as your friends and family, as much as your romantic one." He sighs. "I know that's probably not the right thing to say, but I care about you and want to make sure you do what's best for you. So, I want to remind you that romance isn't everything. Romance is incredible, like what I had with your mom, but there are so many other amazing relationships in life, like the connection I have with you two and all my life-long friends."

I stare at him for a few long moments, unsure if I should smile or cry. Part of me feels annoyed that he's making soulmates seem less significant. But the other part of me realizes that he's right. I love spending time with him, Liz, Rory, and all the other people in my life. I don't want a romantic relationship to get in the way of that.

Okay, maybe part of me still does. Part of me will always wish that I'll get a fairy tale romance story. But as time goes on, I realize more and more that it isn't a realistic dream.

"Mila, please say something," he says. "I'm not trying to be mean. I just worry that your mom hyped up SoulSearchers too much, but I won't do that. I want you to be happy with or without a soulmate. And since I'm guessing you still really want to fall in love, I really hope you find a great partner. Just please don't rush the process. I don't want to see you sacrifice your happiness trying to find love."

I nod. "Thank you, Dad. I know you're right, but it's hard for me to process. I really want to find true love. I want something magical like what you and mom had. But you're right. I can still find happiness in other areas of my life while I look for love."

He smiles. "Exactly. And if you ever need someone to talk to, I'm here for you."

"I am too," Liz says, gently nudging me with her shoulder. "Just in case you want to talk about girly things that Dad won't understand."

I laugh and turn back to my dad. "And I just want to let you know that I did want something romantic to happen between me and Rory. But Liz kept telling me that I should be focusing on a friendship instead of something more. I think you saying that has opened my eyes to what Liz has been warning me of. Rory is an amazing friend, and I don't want my obsession with soulmates to ruin that."

"That's great, Mila," my dad says. "I hope I'll be able to meet Rory soon. She sounds like a good person to have in your life."

"Yeah, she really is." This time, when I talk about Rory, I'm not picturing hearts floating around her. I'm thinking about all the fun activities we've done together as friends. My dad is right. That bond is important, but it doesn't have to be romantic to be something special.

Chapter Fourteen
Mila

The party decorations make our apartment magical. Sparkly streamers hang from every corner, balloons are tied to our furniture, and the beautiful rainbow cake that Rory dropped off is the finishing touch as the table centerpiece.

I glance at Liz, who's reading a piece of paper at the table. Liz has never been one to adore all the glitz and glamor of a birthday party, but she's usually a bit more outgoing and bubbly once the party approaches. Last year, she had a gorgeous blue party dress and a tiara. This year, she's wearing shorts and a lacy tank top. It's cute, but it's not much different than her normal wardrobe.

I consider saying something. After all, I don't want to outshine her in my pink sequin dress. But she has been staring at that paper for so long that I don't think she's even reading it. Something else is going on in her head.

I cautiously pull out a chair and sit in the seat across from her. The cake between us is tempting, but I promised Rory we'd save it until the party started.

"Sorry, I was just looking at the list of guests you gave me. Did you really invite this many people? You do know the size of our apartment, right?" she asks.

I lean forward and look at the list. "Yeah, it's longer than normal, but I wanted to go big this year. I'm sure some of them won't show up. It'll be great!"

Liz sighs. "Mila, you don't even hang out with most of these people."

"I don't need to hang out with someone all the time to invite them to a party."

"I know, but look at some of these. Christine? Have you talked to her since high school?"

"This will be a good excuse for us to catch up."

She peels her eyes away from the paper long enough to look me up and down. "Look, I don't care who you invite and don't invite, but I just wish we had talked about this more before the day of. I don't want our neighbors to complain about the noise."

"Well, good thing I invited the neighbors."

Liz rolls her eyes. "I know I said I wouldn't bother you about this anymore, but does this long list have anything to do with Rory?"

"Rory? Yeah, she's an extra person on the list who wasn't there last year."

"No, what I mean is... are you inviting all these people to make yourself seem cooler for Rory?"

"Why would I do that? She'd still be my friend even if I didn't have a lot of other friends." Because let's face it, I don't have any other close friends right now. I grew apart from most of them, and the ones I occasionally see never seem that interested in spending time with me or hearing about all my dog adventures.

"Liz, I know I was crazy about Rory romantically in the past, but I'm over that now," I remind her. I hesitate for a moment. "And okay, maybe I initially invited more friends to seem cooler, but after talking to Dad yesterday, I realized that it's okay for her to just be my friend. Having a good friend right now might even be better for me than a partner."

Liz's face softens. "Oh. I'm really happy to hear that. I'm glad you've found a friend like her."

I smile, but before I can respond, someone rings the doorbell. I glance at the clock and frown. The party doesn't start for another 40 minutes.

I stand up before Liz can. "I'll get it. I'm not sure who thinks it's normal to come this early."

Before I open the door, I look through the peephole. My heart freezes. I glance at Liz with wide eyes. "Actually, I think you should get it. If you want."

"Huh?" Liz gets up and gently shoves me out of the way to look through the peephole. When she sees who it is, she gasps, and her puzzled expression turns to anger.

I quickly back away as she yanks the door open so fast that it slams against the wall. Standing on the other side of the door is Sawyer, wearing a purple dress shirt and khakis as if he's about to attend a nice party.

Liz shakes her head. "Sawyer, I didn't invite you to my party!"

"I know, I know," he says. "I heard about it from one of your friends. I figured it would be a good time to talk since you're usually in a good mood before these things."

"I would be in a much better mood if you weren't here. You had weeks to talk to me, and you didn't until now? Right before I have all my friends come over? What is wrong with you?"

"Can I please just come in?" he asks. "I'm really sorry for how I acted."

Liz glances at me out of the corner of her eye. I shrug, not sure what she expects from me. If I were her, I'd at least hear him out, but I have no idea what she's thinking.

"Fine," Liz says after several uncomfortable moments.

Sawyer enters the apartment cautiously as Liz closes the door behind him. He stands in the entryway, avoiding eye contact with both of us.

"Go ahead. Talk. I have a party in a half hour," Liz mutters.

"Well, I just wanted to say how sorry I am. I still want to be with you," he says.

Liz crosses her arms. Her face doesn't soften at all. "Why did it take you so long to come to that conclusion?"

"I just needed time to think. It really broke my heart when I heard that you didn't love me from the beginning. But I still have a hard time believing that's true. We were such a good match even back then."

"Wow, I can't believe I was expecting a real apology. How could I love you so early on if I barely even knew you?"

"Because we're soulmates. That's just how it works."

"No, you can't just be soulmates. You actually have to get to know each other and put in the work if you want the relationship to be successful."

"Well, I'm putting in the work now."

"You're really not. And honestly, it's too late for you to start giving a shit. I'm not getting back together with you no matter what you say."

"What the hell do you mean? We never broke up!"

"When my boyfriend stops talking to me for weeks for a petty reason, that's definitely a breakup. I don't want to be with someone who only wants to be better when the relationship is at risk."

Sawyer takes a step back, but instead of leaving, he turns to me. "Come on, Mila. Tell her she's being crazy. You know how important soulmates are."

For once, I'm speechless. He knows love is my weak spot. But when I glance at my sister, who's standing tall and speaking her mind, I don't feel sad that the relationship is ending. I'm proud of her for staying true to herself.

I shake my head. "No, Sawyer, you're the one who's crazy. It doesn't matter if you were 'meant to be' with my sister if you're not going to treat her right."

His jaw drops. He's used to me trying to stay positive when it comes to partners disagreeing. But not anymore.

"Sawyer, please get out of my apartment," Liz says.

"Come on, Liz. We're soulmates. We have the SoulSearchers to prove it."

He pulls his SoulSearcher out of his pocket and puts it on his wrist. It lights up, but only faintly. Liz narrows her eyes and storms off to her room. She comes back with her SoulSearcher, which is also a bracelet.

Normally, Liz's bracelet vibrates when she's next to her soulmate. Yet, in her hands right now, nothing happens. It just looks like an ordinary piece of jewelry.

Sawyer's smug expression slowly fades when he realizes what this means. But he doesn't back away. Instead, he shakes his head and furrows his brow, trying not to look phased. "Well, that's because you're not wearing it."

Liz wasn't wearing it when she met Sawyer. It was tied to her backpack like a keychain, but it still vibrated. Sawyer must remember that, but the desperation in his eyes suggests that he's willing to try anything at this point.

Liz rolls her eyes and puts the bracelet on. Nothing happens, even while she's staring directly at Sawyer.

"See?" Liz says. "Is this good enough proof that we shouldn't be together?"

"Wait, are you only breaking up with me because your SoulSearcher is broken? That's ridiculous," Sawyer says. "You should at least take it in to make sure this isn't a mistake."

"I had no idea that it wouldn't vibrate. I was actually planning to smash it if it did, but I suppose this is more civil. The point is, maybe you were my soulmate at one point, but I know you're not anymore. In fact, I don't think you're mature enough to be anyone's soulmate right now."

"What the hell? I'm older than you!"

"Age and maturity don't always go hand in hand."

Suddenly, Sawyer bursts into a rant filled with swears that I'm not comfortable repeating. His face turns red and he clenches his fists as he yells. I reach out and grab Liz's hand, forcing her to take a step back in case he starts swinging.

But, luckily, he doesn't. When neither of us react to his outburst, he eventually stops yelling. He converts his words into an intense glare. "You're going to regret this, Liz. I'm going to find someone way hotter than you and then you'll be begging me to take you back."

Liz crosses her arms and scoffs. "Yeah, okay then. I do hope you find someone that's better for you one day. Just please don't do it out of spite."

"Stop trying to have the last word," Sawyer yells before storming out the front door, leaving Liz and I to let out a sigh of relief.

I hug Liz briefly before breaking away to read her expression. She seems surprisingly calm considering the intense events that just occurred. "Liz, are you okay? I can't believe he was that harsh with you, especially since he was the one who avoided you for weeks."

Instead of sobbing or panicking, Liz laughs. She actually laughs. "I'm absolutely fine. What an idiot! I'm glad he showed his true colors before I dated him any longer."

"You're not sad that it didn't work out?"

"Hell no. I'd rather be single for the rest of my life than have to put up with that any longer."

I laugh with her, but I admire her bravery. Being single forever is a fear I've been ignoring lately, but suddenly, I'm reminded that this is yet another birthday party without a soulmate.

"Anyway, let's finish getting ready," Liz says. "I'm not going to let him ruin our celebration."

"I agree." After all that, I'm extra excited to start drinking and partying.

Chapter Fifteen
Rory

The parking lot at Mila's apartment complex is packed as I near her unit. I circle around a few times until I finally find a spot where I don't have to parallel park. It's not that I can't parallel park, but I'll feel super awkward if I hold up the cars behind me while doing so. When I finally get out of my car and walk toward her place, I can hear music from outside her door. I hate to be a party pooper, but I worry about their poor neighbors.

Only seconds after I knock on the door, it flies open. Mila stands there with a massive smile. "Rory, you made it!"

She leans forward and hugs me tightly. It's only about a half hour since the party started, but I can tell that Mila is at least a little drunk already. I wasn't sure what type of party it was, so I tried not to come too early or too late.

"Of course I came," I say when she finally pulls away. "I told you I would."

I glance around the apartment curiously as Mila closes the door behind me. The space is packed! There are people in every corner chatting with a drink in their hand. The table is full of a few people playing a card game as several others watch while eating the cake I made.

Suddenly, my body freezes and the walls feel uncomfortably close. Everywhere I look, there are strangers. I love spending time with Mila, but large crowds are not my thing. Part of me had hoped that this would be more of a casual game night sort of party, but loud music and drinks it is. I try to calculate how long I should stay. Maybe I'll let Mila introduce me to a few people and then sneak out. Or maybe I'll stick it out longer if I can hide in the corner and pet Kiki.

Mila snaps me out of my panic by grabbing my wrist and leading me into the kitchen. "Can I get you anything to drink? And if you want some cake, it's delicious! Someone awesome made it." She nudges me playfully as she says it.

I laugh nervously. Not because I don't think she's funny but because someone behind me keeps bumping me with their elbow and they don't even seem to care. "Just water is fine for now."

Mila nods and disappears for a moment as she pours a cup of water. She hands it to me with a big smile across her face. I force a smile back as sweat builds on my forehead.

"So, are all these people your friends? I'm surprised I've never met them before," I say.

"Yeah, some are my friends and some are Liz's. We're both pretty popular."

I wait for her to introduce me to someone, but she doesn't. She's busy dancing to the music as she sips a drink. I glance around, looking for Kiki. Unfortunately, she's already surrounded by a crowd of people petting her.

"Well, I should probably go say hi to Liz before I forget. She's the only other person here that I know, after all." I don't want to leave Mila's side, but I have no idea what else to say. I can barely hear her above the music, and I feel completely out of my element.

Mila grabs my wrist again before I can move. "Rory, wait! Don't go. I know this is probably a lot for you. Do you want to step out on the patio and get some fresh air?"

I glance over at the small screened-in patio at the other side of the apartment. No one else is out there right now, so I eagerly nod. "Yeah, that sounds wonderful."

Mila guides me toward the patio with her hand still around my wrist. I don't shake her hand away because I know her guiding me is better than me bumping into random people. Mila doesn't stumble at all on her way there, so maybe she's not as drunk as I thought.

As we step outside, we're greeted with a warm breeze. Mila finally lets go of me and sinks into one of the cushioned patio chairs. I sit on the one beside her.

"Are you enjoying your party so far?" I ask.

At first, she smiles and nods, but after she processes my question a bit more, she hesitates. "Honestly, no. I used to love partying, but every year, I feel like I have fewer friends that I enjoy partying with."

"Well, everyone here seems really nice," I say, even though I obviously haven't interacted with anyone yet. They all look nice from afar, I guess.

She sighs. "They are nice, but I'm not as close to them as I've made it seem. I haven't hung out with a lot of them in years, but I thought having a long guest list would make me seem cool."

"Well, that's silly. The number of friends you have isn't what makes you cool."

"Then what makes me cool?"

"You're fun to be around. You do a lot of good things for animals in need. To me, those things are way cooler than hosting a crowded party."

"Huh. I never thought about it like that." She takes a sip of her drink. "Are you sure you're not just saying that to make me feel better?"

"I'm certain. I don't like big parties, so normally, I would leave immediately if I arrived at a place this crowded. However, you've been a really good friend to me, so this party is an exception."

"You really never had a party phase in your teens? You look like you'd be popular."

"Absolutely not. I spent most of high school reading instead of socializing."

She smiles. "That's okay. Being popular in high school is overrated anyway."

I nod, but neither of us continue the conversation. So, I decide that it's the right time to pull out the birthday present. I unzip my purse-sized backpack and touch the gift to make sure it's still in there. Of course, it is.

"Hey, is now a good time to give you your present?"

Her eyes light up. "Wait, you got me a present? You know you didn't have to, right? This is just a party, it's not my actual birthday."

"I know, but it's the first time I'm celebrating your birthday with you, so I wanted to get you something to thank you for being so kind to me."

I pull out a pink envelope and hand it to her. A paw print sticker seals it. As I pass it to her, I worry she'll be disappointed that the package isn't bigger. But she grins from ear to ear.

"It's okay if I open it now?"

"Yes, of course." But I hold my breath, praying that I chose the gift wisely.

Without hesitating, she tears the envelope open, not bothering to do it neatly. She slides out the paper that's inside and unfolds it. I watch as she examines it for a few minutes. That's probably my cue to explain the purpose of this uncommon gift.

"I spent a lot of time trying to figure out the perfect gift for you, and none of the typical things made sense," I say. "So, I sponsored a rescue dog on your behalf. His name is Felix, and he's a senior Pit Bull. I paid for his full adoption fee so he can get adopted faster. I figured helping a dog would be more meaningful to you than any item ever could."

She studies the paper for a few more excruciating moments. I begin to worry that she hates it. Sure, she loves animals, but would she have preferred something for herself? Did she want a physical object?

"Wait, but adoption fees can be like hundreds of dollars sometimes," she says without looking up from the paper.

"Well, yeah, but this dog really needs a home, so the price wasn't important to me."

Mila's blue eyes look up at me, and I notice tears forming. I'm about to ask if they're happy or sad tears, but before I can say a word, she leans forward and hugs me as tightly as possible. I'm surprised to find myself leaning into the hug.

"You like it?" I ask once I pull away.

"Rory, of course! This is the most thoughtful gift anyone has ever given me. Knowing a dog was saved on my behalf is so much better than something that would just sit and collect dust."

I smile, feeling extra grateful that I didn't buy a necklace. "That's what I thought. I'm so happy I trusted my gut."

She nods. "I know how we met isn't ideal, but this proves that you're the closest friend I have right now. You really get me."

I can't stop smiling. I'm a little embarrassed to admit that I haven't felt this close to someone since I was a little kid. Then again, approaching new people and sharing my feelings seemed much easier when I was younger.

The room lights up a bit. At first, I assume someone turned the porch light on. But Mila's expression morphs into an emotion I've never seen before. If there was a step above pure joy, that would be the best way to describe it. She gasps and her eyes sparkle.

Before I can ask, she leans forward as if she's about to hug me again. But it's not a hug, and I don't realize it until it's too late. She kisses me right on the lips. It feels disgusting! I immediately feel bad for thinking that of Mila, but to be fair, I think that's how any kiss would feel to me.

I haven't kissed anyone since I was 18 or 19, when I was still trying to figure out my sexuality, but it's just as bad as I remember it. Who thought the idea of mashing two people's mouths together was appealing?

The kiss only lasts for a second because I push her off as soon as I fully process what's happening. "Mila! What the hell was that?"

Her ecstatic expression vanishes immediately, but she doesn't look completely defeated. Just a little puzzled. She gestures to my wrist. "Your SoulSearcher lit up! We really are soulmates."

I glance down at my SoulSearcher bracelet, and sure enough, it's shining as bright as Mila's had on the day we met. I've only been wearing it because I know it makes Mila happy, but after that awful kiss, I'm certain wearing it was a mistake.

"Look, I understand if you're not ready to kiss or anything. I'm so sorry. I shouldn't have rushed that. I was just so excited!" Mila says. "All this time, Liz kept insisting that I stop wishing for anything romantic with you, and I was finally happy with being in the friend zone. But now that your SoulSearcher is glowing, it's okay for me to embrace the feelings I have for you. We really are soulmates!"

I scoot my chair back and shake my head. "No, what are you talking about? I made it very clear that I couldn't be romantically or sexually attracted to anyone. That hasn't changed."

"What do you mean? Of course it has changed. Your SoulSearcher lit up!"

I glance down at the bracelet one more time. It's still glowing, but I shake my head.

"So? You're going to listen to a silly bracelet instead of your friend?" I ask.

Mila stands up quickly. "It's not a silly bracelet! It's a *SoulSearcher*. And why would it light up if we weren't destined to be in a relationship?"

"I don't know! I have the same information you do," I say. Of course, I'm confused about the reason behind it too, but I know how I feel. "Maybe the system has evolved to match people in other ways. Maybe it lit up because we're destined to be in each other's lives, just not like that. Friend soulmates."

"That's not how it works. Friend soulmates aren't a thing."

"And why not?"

"Because the SoulSearcher is supposed to lead me to love. And if it will never do that, then what's the point?" A tear drips down her cheek.

"No one is saying you can't find love. I can be in your life as your best friend *and* you can fall in love with someone else. The two are not mutually exclusive."

"But I want to be in love with you."

Now I'm the one with tears in my eyes. I try my best to blink them away, but one escapes. I take a deep breath. "Does our friendship really mean that little to you? I thought you had gotten over expecting romance with me, but as soon as you think there's a chance, you throw away everything we've built as friends to pursue love instead. I care about you a lot and I want to be your friend, but I'm never going to be interested in you as a partner."

Mila continues to cry as she clenches her fists. "Well, I don't want to be friends with you then! I want to find love, and all you're doing is preventing me from that."

"Mila, I know you don't mean that."

"I do mean it! Because if you won't love me even when your SoulSearcher says you're meant to, then what's the point? If this is just a friendship, then it's distracting me from finding what I really care about."

I flinch as she says "just" a friendship. As if a friendship can't be fulfilling like romance can. I open my mouth to speak, but she's already storming back inside and slamming the patio door behind her.

I get up and rush after Mila. Once I'm back in the apartment, I see her sparkly pink dress headed for the front door. "Mila, wait! You're obviously drunk, so please don't drive."

"I'm not an idiot. I'll walk or call a rideshare if I have to. I just need to get out of here," she calls back to me without turning around. Everyone near the front door turns to look at her with wide eyes, but the music is so loud that most of the guests don't even notice her outburst.

She slams the door behind her. I know she wants space, but I need to know that she's okay, so I follow.

But by the time I race outside, she's nowhere to be seen.

Chapter Sixteen
Mila

"Hi, am I in the right place? I need to get my SoulSearcher fixed," I say as I slam the necklace on the counter in front of me.

The lady working is in a cozy-looking office chair, flipping through a magazine. When she gets to an acceptable stopping point in her reading, she sets the magazine on the counter and meets my gaze. "Of course. What seems to be the problem?"

"It matched me with someone who's asexual and aromantic. She doesn't love me. You need to fix this now!"

She sighs. "Well, that's not something we can instantly fix."

"What do you mean? This place is called the SoulSearcher Help Center. So, shouldn't your job be to help me?"

"Look, I'm just an employee here. I have nothing to do with how the SoulSearchers are programmed. This is a very complicated problem. My job is to answer questions or fix a broken wire, not to change who your soulmate is."

"But people change soulmates all the time. There are so many movies and books about it."

"You know movies and books aren't always realistic, right?" Ugh, she sounds like Liz. I have so much I want to say, but I keep my mouth shut because it's clearly a rhetorical question. "But yes, you can change your soulmate. However, it's up to the system, not up to you. If your match mentioned in her questionnaire that she doesn't want to be matched with someone, then I'm sure they're already working on matching you with someone new. Just in case it's not on their radar yet, I can flag your profile to let them know."

"And then what?"

"Be patient. Eventually, your SoulSearcher will link to someone who's more compatible with you."

"Be patient? But how long will that take?"

"I can't give you a clear answer. Sometimes, there's a good fit right away, but other times, it takes a while."

"A while? What, like months? Or years? I can't wait for years! I already waited so long to get a match and that obviously was a waste of time. I want someone to love me now."

"Look, you're not the first person to deal with this. Making a note in your account is really all I can do to speed up the process. And even then, they can't speed it up if there's not a good match for you at this point in time."

I shudder at the thought of being alone for years. What if they never find another good match for me? What if all the good matches are already taken and never become available again? Will I die as an old, lonely lady?

"There must be something else I can do, right?" I hesitate for a moment before acknowledging the obvious solution. "Like, do you think it would be faster for me to find love without the SoulSearcher?"

She taps her fingers on the counter as if I'm wasting her time. But it's the middle of the night and no one else is here, so what else could she possibly have to do? "Sure, you can turn in your SoulSearcher. Lots of people find love without it, but those relationships typically aren't as solid. It's a lot of extra work too."

I consider that option for a moment. While going out and finding love the old-fashioned way had never been my plan, I could make it work. As long as someone loves me, everything else will sort itself out. Right?

"Are there really enough people out there not using a SoulSearcher?" I ask.

She nods without meeting my gaze. "While taking the SoulSearcher route is certainly the most common, there are plenty of people who never use one. And there are also lots of people who have turned their SoulSearchers in after having issues with them or not wanting them anymore."

"But how can I find those people? I'm sure they're not walking around telling everyone that the soulmate system failed them. That would be silly."

I swear she rolls her eyes when she thinks I'm not looking. "We have an online platform for people who have decided to get rid of their SoulSearchers so they can connect with each other and find love easier. We still want to set them up for success, after all," she explains, but her voice is monotone. "And you can request your SoulSearcher back in the future. But whenever it's in our possession, it won't be actively finding you a soulmate."

"Thanks, that helps," I say. But it really comes down to one aspect: which method will be the fastest? It seems obvious to me, despite how overwhelming it is.

The woman glances at her magazine out of the corner of her eye, clearly longing to read it some more. "Why don't you take some time to think about it and come back once you've decided?"

I shake my head and slide my necklace closer to her. "I don't need time to think about it. I want to turn it in so I can find my soulmate now."

She glances at the piece of jewelry and furrows her brow. "Are you sure? This is a big decision. And since it looks like you just came from some wild party, I'm guessing you're not thinking clearly."

"I am sure. I've never been more sure in my life." The idea of going out and dating other people in a similar boat as me is actually starting to sound appealing. I've never been on a real date before, and I've wanted to so badly. Now, it's finally time.

She locks eyes with me for a moment and sighs. Then, she reaches out and takes the necklace away.

Chapter Seventeen
Rory

"Thanks for coming over. You really didn't have to," I say. Zaya sits next to me on my couch with Minnie curled up in her lap. Tyson walks a few steps out of his crate to glance at us from around the corner, but as soon as Zaya looks at him, he darts away.

After everything that went down with Mila, I had no idea who to talk to. Zaya was the only person I could think of who would understand, especially since this wasn't something I wanted to bring up in front of the whole support group.

"Of course, I did. It sounds like you're going through a lot and I want to help," she says as Minnie flops over for a belly rub. "I know I can't make Mila talk to you, but I'm happy to listen and offer advice as needed. Have you heard from her at all yet?"

"No, I texted her after it happened last night, but I took the hint when she never responded. I figured I'd give her some space for a few days to let her cool down."

Zaya nods. "Yeah, that's a good idea. I'm sure she just needs some time to come to her senses."

"So, you're not going to try to talk me out of being friends with her?"

"No, why would I do that?"

"Because you've always seemed very skeptical about my relationship with her, especially when I first talked about it at the support group."

"I just wanted to make sure neither of you got hurt. But now, I can see that you really care about her, so if you still want her in your life, I respect your decision," she says. "How she treated you at that party wasn't okay at all, but sadly, I can understand where she's coming from."

"You can?" I never thought someone on the asexual spectrum would relate to someone as love-obsessed as Mila. But then again, I often forget that not every asexual person is also aromantic like me.

"Absolutely. When I was younger, I was crazy about finding love too. That's why I stayed with Aero, the first person I was matched with, for so long. I was determined to make it work because I believed in love so much. It took me a long time to realize that being in a relationship can do more harm than good if that person isn't right for you." She sighs. "It seems like Mila is going through something similar. She wants so badly for her first soulmate to work out that she hasn't realized she's hurting herself and you in the process."

"Wow, I'm sorry you went through that. And I guess it helps me understand where Mila is coming from a little better. Obviously, I'm hurt by some of the things she said, but I don't think she ever had malicious intentions." I pause for a second. "Wait, your ex's name is Aero? Like Aro? Aromantic?"

Zaya laughs. "Yeah, it's pretty weird, right? Trust me, he's not aromantic or asexual at all. Quite the opposite, actually."

I chuckle and glance at the floor. "Anyway, I know I need to give Mila space, but is it bad that I'm worried about her? I just want to know if she's okay. I don't think she drove last night, but she was a little drunk, so what if something bad happened?"

"Rory, take a deep breath. I'm sure she's okay, but if you're really worried, maybe ask her sister instead of reaching out to her directly? You did say she has a sister, right?"

"Yeah, that's a good idea." I pick up my phone and scroll through my contacts, trying to remember if I ever saved Liz's number. Luckily, it's in there. Although I don't know if I've ever used it before. What if Liz doesn't want to talk to me either? "Do you mind if I call her quick?"

"Not at all! I'll just be over here petting Minnie." She glances over to see if Tyson wants to join them, but of course, he doesn't.

"Thank you," I say as I walk over to the furthest corner of the apartment. Since my apartment isn't very spacious, I know she'll be able to hear everything I say, but I don't have many other options. I guess I could step outside, but then my neighbors could eavesdrop, which might be worse. Ugh, I hate making phone calls.

I stare at Liz's contact information for a few seconds before clicking "call" to rip off the band-aid. As I hold the phone to my ear, a million thoughts rush through my mind, but I try my best to ignore them.

"Hello?" a tired voice answers. It's the afternoon of the day after the party, but it makes sense that Liz would be exhausted. I left right after the situation with Mila, but the party might've gone on all night.

"Hi, is this Liz?"

"Yeah, who is this?"

"It's Rory." I pause to see if she has any reaction to my name, but she doesn't. "I'm sorry for calling out of the blue, but I just wanted to make sure Mila is okay."

"Um, I'm not really sure. She disappeared before the party was over and she went straight to her room when she got home late last night. All I got from her was a text saying, 'I'm going to fix my SoulSearcher. Don't worry about me.' Honestly, I am a little worried though."

On one hand, Mila is safe. I'm glad she's home. But on the other hand, she was so upset with me that she rushed to get a soulmate. That doesn't make me feel good, but hopefully, she finds what she needs.

"She didn't tell you what happened?" I ask.

"No, why? Did something happen between you two?"

Oh, boy. I wasn't expecting to be the one to tell Liz about this, but she deserves to know. So, I tell her everything I can remember about last night, up until the point where Mila disappeared and hasn't spoken to me since.

"Wow," Liz says. "I'm sorry she's acting like that. I kept telling her to stop thinking about you as more than a friend, but she wouldn't listen."

"It's okay. I'm sure she's dealing with a lot right now."

"You're not mad at her? I'd be furious if I found out my best friend would willingly throw away my friendship to pursue love."

"Part of me is frustrated with her, but I'm sure if we just talked it out, everything would be okay. Can you keep me updated with how she's doing?"

"Yeah, of course. And if you need anything, don't hesitate to reach out to me. I know we're not really friends, but I've gotten used to having you around. I'd hate to see you and Mila drift apart."

"Thanks, Liz. I appreciate it."

After I hang up, I walk back into the living room to find Zaya throwing a squeaky toy around as Minnie chases it. Whenever Minnie picks it up, she makes Zaya wrestle with her to get it back.

Zaya looks up at me. "Did talking to her sister help?"

"I think so, but only time will tell."

To my surprise, Tyson inches out of his crate far enough to sniff my leg. Maybe he can sense that I'm having a bad day and wants to cheer me up. As soon as I look at him, he disappears into his crate again with wide, scared eyes.

He sure is one unusual dog, but I have to say, I relate to him in some ways.

Chapter Eighteen
Mila

I've heard many stories about SoulSearcher-less dating, but it always sounded complicated and frustrating. People can still meet at bars and use dating apps, but I don't know of any successful relationships that started that way. Those methods are typically for casual dating rather than finding a life partner.

However, now that I'm in a position to date without a SoulSearcher, I'm actually finding it intriguing. The online platform I gained access to after turning in my SoulSearcher is like a mix between a social media site and a dating app. I can communicate with other people in the same boat as me. When I first signed in, it asked me to set my preferences, such as age, gender, and location.

Right away, I made a post on the site to introduce myself and let everyone know what I was looking for. I was surprised how many people commented on the post within a few hours. (All men, despite me setting my posts to be available to any gender).

This site has made me understand the appeal of online dating. It makes me feel wanted. Whenever someone comments on my post or messages me, I have access to their profile. There are so many options, and looking through all the profiles is addicting. With the SoulSearcher, I knew there was only one person out there for me, but now, I can choose anyone I want! Well, as long as they like me back. But so far, it seems like every guy likes me.

I've responded to nearly every personal message I've received and sent a message to anyone commenting on my post. As long as their profile is interesting enough, I don't see why I shouldn't give them a chance. Being picky would only make it harder for me to find someone to be with. I've been having a lot of great conversations with people, but many of them stopped responding after a while or weren't looking for something serious.

But eventually, I met someone I instantly connected with. His first message just said, "hey, ur cute!" which might sound lame to some people, but it made me blush uncontrollably. I couldn't remember the last time someone had flirted with me or called me cute.

I clicked on his profile, and luckily, I found him super attractive. His name is Aero and he's only a few years older than me. I can't understand why a young, good-looking guy like him wouldn't have a soulmate by now. Although, to be fair, I'm also an attractive young person without someone to love me, so maybe his situation is like mine.

I was flattered that Aero reached out to me first. I couldn't stop looking at his cute profile photo. So, after only a few messages back and forth, I agreed to meet him. That's where I am now; waiting at a restaurant for him to show up. He said we were meeting at six for dinner, but now it's five minutes past that. For a brief moment, I wonder if he's ghosting me, but I shake that nonsense out of my mind.

"Mila?" a voice behind me says, but they pronounce it as My-luh instead of Mee-luh.

I turn around to see Aero standing there, holding a bouquet of roses. I'm pleased to see that he looks just like his picture. In fact, he's even more handsome in person.

"Aero! It's nice to meet you." I reach out to shake his hand but he pulls me in for a hug, which makes me feel warm and fuzzy inside. "Also, my name is Mila." I pronounce it right so he doesn't have to embarrass himself again.

When he pulls away from the hug, he stares at my face lovingly. His brown eyes and long eyelashes are gorgeous, but I try not to stare. "Sorry if that was too forward," he says. "I'm so excited to finally see you in person."

I find it interesting that he says 'finally' even though we only started talking 24 hours ago. But I appreciate his enthusiasm. He's interested in me the way that I'd hoped Rory would be. And he's exactly my type. He reminds me a little of "Axel," the imaginary soulmate I always pictured. He has the same dark hair and clean-shaven face I'd always daydreamed about.

He holds out the roses to me. "These are for you." I blush and take them without hesitation. No one has ever bought me flowers before, but it has always been a fantasy of mine.

"Thank you so much! I love them."

A waitress leads us to a table by the window, where I can see lots of people walking down the sidewalk, many of them with dogs. I have the urge to squeal with excitement every time I see a dog, so I can't stay quiet. "Oh my goodness, look at all the cute dogs outside!"

He's already looking at the menu, so he only glances out of the corner of his eye. "Oh, I'm actually more of a cat person."

My heart sinks a tiny bit. But being a cat person doesn't automatically mean he hates dogs, so I'll give him the benefit of the doubt.

"Oh, do you have a cat?"

He shakes his head. "No, but I've been considering it for a while. I had cats growing up and I love how independent they are while still being playful. What about you? Do you have any pets?"

"No cats, but I do have an adorable dog named Kiki," I say. "I'm sure you saw this on my profile, but I adore both dogs and cats since I work at an animal shelter."

"You work at an animal shelter? Don't you mean volunteer?"

"No, I'm one of the few employees there. It doesn't pay a ton, but it's enough to get by, and I love helping animals in need." Did he not read my profile? I had studied his very closely. He works in the tech industry and seems to be very wealthy for his age. He has also lived in Tampa his whole life, and he's into anime and video games. "I'm also a certified dog trainer, so I'll sometimes train dogs in my free time to earn extra cash."

"Well, what's your plan for the future?" Despite being such a big question, he's still scanning the menu very closely.

"What do you mean? This is my plan. Maybe not exactly this because the shelter and training both take up a lot of time, but I'll always do work that helps animals."

Finally, he puts down his menu and looks into my eyes. He smiles. "That's cool that you're so passionate."

He gazes at me in a way that makes me want to melt, making me forget what we were even talking about. I wait for him to ask me another question, but when he doesn't, I decide to get an important topic out of the way. "What made you get rid of your SoulSearcher?"

His eyes widen, but he chuckles. "Wow, we're just going to get right to it then?"

"We talked about mine over text, so it's only fair."

"Right. Well, my situation was actually very similar. I got matched with someone, and I thought we were deeply in love. But she never seemed as attracted to me as I was to her. Eventually, she ended it. It broke my heart, so I decided to find my next match without the SoulSearcher."

"Oh, I'm sorry she did that to you. That explains why you're so handsome yet still single."

He laughs. "I know I'm good-looking, but you're gorgeous. I couldn't believe it when you messaged me back. You're way out of my league."

My face turns bright red. He must be saying that just to be nice, right? I'm not out of anyone's league. Sure, I'm cute, but I'm just a normal person.

He smirks. "You're not used to people complimenting you, are you?"

"No, I'm definitely not used to it." I giggle as I speak. "It's a weird feeling, but I like it."

"Good. I will always do everything I can to make you feel special."

The blushing continues, but then, I realize he used the word always. That's a big word to use so early on, but I'm glad he said it. "You already know you want to keep seeing me? Even though you just met me?"

"Of course! There's just something about you that I'm drawn to. So, you must be my real soulmate."

Could he be right? If both of our SoulSearchers were working, would we be matched together? These butterflies in my stomach definitely say so.

As we order and get our food, we continue to talk and get to know each other. I learn all sorts of random facts about him. He may not be a crazy dog person like me, but in addition to liking cats, he has always dreamed of getting a pet lizard. He has a brother who's deaf, so he's fluent in American Sign Language. He loves food and is always willing to eat, even if he just had lunch. He proves that last fact by cleaning my plate when I only eat half of my meal.

When the waitress brings us the bill, he doesn't hesitate to hand over his card. I don't believe men should always pay for dates, but it feels good to be cared for.

After we exit the restaurant, he pauses a few steps from the front door, so I stop beside him. As he turns to face me, my heart beats faster. I'm about to tell him what a great time I had, but before I can say anything, he leans forward and kisses me! I kiss him back, of course.

The kiss feels weird. I had never kissed anyone before Rory because I wanted to save my first kiss for my soulmate. All that waiting had given me a lot of high expectations. But the reality is that kissing is weird, and it doesn't feel like how you'd picture it. I'm not saying my kiss with Aero was bad, but it might take a while for me to get used to it.

I hope he gives me the chance to get used to it.

After we break apart, I find myself staring into his eyes longingly. They shimmer under the streetlights.

"Mila, I like you a lot, and I don't want this date to end."

I love the way it sounds when he says my name. "Me neither."

Our faces are so close that I swear we're about to kiss again. But something about being so close without actually kissing is almost more intense than the kiss itself.

"Why don't you come back to my place?" he asks.

"Sure, did you have something in mind?" I mean it in an innocent way, such as watching a movie or playing a card game. But judging by the look in his eyes, his intentions are different. So, I try my best to flirt back, despite never really flirting before. "Maybe more kissing?"

He smirks. "Yeah, of course, there will be more kissing. And more than that too."

I try to hide my embarrassment, but my face turns bright red. More than kissing? Is it bad that I had never thought much about what happens after a first kiss? Obviously, I know about sex and all that, but I had never pictured doing it so soon.

I consider leaning into the sexy way he's talking, but I honestly don't feel ready to go too far. "Well, I don't know about all that, but I'd love to hang out with you more. Maybe we could watch a movie or something."

He nods and takes my hand. Our fingers intertwine as we walk toward his car. When we get close enough, he unlocks his car, and I can see that it's incredibly fancy. I don't know anything about cars, but it looks brand new, so I'm sure it's worth like five times what I paid for mine.

"I can drive," he says. "And I'll bring you back to your car later."

I really want to take him up on that offer. It's way more fun to be the passenger. But I know Liz and my dad would be disappointed if I got into a car with someone I just met, even if they were my soulmate. "That's okay, I can follow you there in my car."

Aero doesn't protest, so I hop in my car, set the roses on my passenger seat, and follow him. As we drive, I quickly realize that his place is going to be nothing like mine. His neighborhood isn't far from the restaurant, but it's definitely much fancier than where anyone I know lives. It's a community of condos, and there's a gate that's monitored by a security guard.

When Aero pulls up to the security guard, he talks to them for a few moments, and then the guard waves us both through after opening the gate. I feel like royalty as the gate closes behind my shabby little car. Once I get a closer look at the community, I feel like a peasant. Okay, that's a bit dramatic, but I definitely feel out of place.

Not only are the condos beautiful, but everyone has a nice car like Aero. I see a few people walking Doodles and it takes so much effort for me not to cringe. Don't get me wrong, I think they're adorable just like any other dog, but they don't come from ethical sources. So, it's hard for me to enjoy their cuteness.

Once I stop focusing on the questionable dog choices of this neighborhood, I notice Aero pulling into a garage space marked "residents only." I glance at the outdoor parking spaces next to the garage door, which don't have any signs. I pull into one of those as the garage door closes behind Aero's car.

I sit in my vehicle for a few moments, not sure what to do next. While I'm waiting, I glance down at the bouquet of flowers and smile. I can't wait to display them when I get home.

Aero appears beside my car with an adorable grin on his face. "Welcome to my neighborhood! What do you think?" he says as I hop out of my car.

If he were Rory, I would've made a joke about the Doodles, but I'm not sure if he'd understand. Plus, I don't want him to think I'm a crazy dog lady (which I totally am) because that could scare him off. I'll save all my weird quirks for future dates.

I lock my car and smile. "It's beautiful. I never thought someone my age would be able to afford a place as nice as this."

"Oh, it's not that hard when you have a great job," he chuckles as he speaks, so I fake a laugh too. But I can't help but wonder if it's a dig at my career choice.

He takes my hand, which sends shivers through my body. Then, he leads me to a door that's only a few steps away from my car. I expect the door to open into a hallway or a lobby space, but on the other side is the interior of his condo.

It's like a small house, making my apartment look like a shed. I can't even imagine what he'd think of the size of Rory's place. The entrance opens to a spacious living room, which is next to a dining room with a chandelier-like fixture. To my right, I notice stairs leading to a second story. Along the stairs are large windows that let lots of natural light into the space. It's gorgeous, and I can't help but think about the fact that I could live here one day if he wants to be my soulmate.

"I love this place! Can I get a tour?" I ask.

He puts his arm around me and gazes into my eyes longingly. "We'll have time for that later, but for now, there's one specific room I want to show you."

I expect him to take my hand and lead me there like he has been, but this time, he scoops me up in his arms and carries me up the stairs. I can tell he's struggling a bit, but he doesn't set me down until we enter what I can assume is his bedroom. He tosses me on the bed and then leans over and starts kissing me.

My stomach fills with butterflies. Since I have little experience with kissing, I have never made out with someone before. I do my best to follow his lead and kiss him back.

After a few moments, I feel his hands slide down my body, grazing my boobs along the way. They don't stop until they reach the bottom of my dress. He starts lifting my skirt up, in an effort to pull my dress off, but I quickly leap into defense mode and push him away.

"Sorry," I say. "I don't want to move too fast."

"Too fast? I just wanted to touch your skin."

My face turns red, but my emotions are so confusing. I like the idea of him touching me, but it makes me so scared at the same time. "Well, I've never done anything beyond kissing. So, this is all a little overwhelming for me. I'm not looking to rush."

"Wait, so you're a virgin?" His eyes nearly bulge out of his head when he comes to that realization. I hate how people are always surprised when they learn this. In a world where you can be matched with a soulmate, you'd think being a virgin in your 20s would be more common than it used to be.

"Well, yeah. Why would I do it with someone who wasn't my soulmate?"

"Just for fun?"

I shake my head. "No, I'm not interested in that. I want my first time to be meaningful. I want it to be with the person I'm going to spend the rest of my life with."

He reaches out and takes my hand. Our fingers intertwine as he squeezes tightly. "Well, I want to be the person you spend the rest of your life with. I think we're meant to be soulmates."

I glance up so my eyes meet his. Wow, he's even more handsome after saying that. He's looking down at me so lovingly as if I'm the most beautiful girl in the world. Obviously, I'd love to be his soulmate. It means I'd never have to spend another day feeling depressed or wondering when my true love will find me. But I don't want to seem as desperate as I feel.

"Are you sure? You don't want to get to know me better first?"

He shakes his head without hesitation. "Mila, I've spent a lot of time trying to find my soulmate, and I've never had a connection as strong as what I'm feeling right now with you. I could see myself falling in love with you, marrying you, and having kids with you. It seems like the perfect future for me, and I hope you feel the same."

"Wow." It's the only word I can get out at first. My heart beats fast and my face feels so hot that I'm worried it will melt. He just said everything I've ever wanted to hear from a person. "That does sound wonderful. And I'd love for us to be soulmates. But I just want to make sure we do this right. Are you sure rushing into a relationship like this is okay with you?"

What is wrong with me? With the SoulSearcher, I was ready to accept anyone as my soulmate if my necklace told me to be with them. Now, I have an actual person confessing their feelings for me and I'm being hesitant? This is what I've always dreamed of! Why am I so scared all of a sudden?

"Sure, it's a bit fast, but if we both know we're a good match, then why wait? Why waste any more time not being soulmates?" Before I can respond, he leans in and kisses me. It's a long, passionate kiss. The kind you see in romance movies.

When he pulls away, he gazes at me lovingly again. "So, what do you say? Will you be my girlfriend?"

There's no way I can say no to that! This is like one of my wildest dreams coming to life before my eyes. A massive grin appears on my face as I lean forward to hug him as tightly as I can. "Absolutely! I'd love to."

He smiles from ear to ear too, and within seconds, we're making out again. But this time, I don't try to stop him when he pulls off my dress. He is my soulmate, after all.

Chapter Nineteen
Rory

Tyson sits on the couch next to me. Well, sort of next to me. He's on one end while I'm on the other. But he still jumped onto the couch while I was already sitting here, so it's a huge milestone for my timid foster dog.

I stay frozen in place. I know even the smallest movement could scare him off, so I become a statue. Although, I wish I had turned on the TV first. I guess I'll just have to sit in place until Tyson gets comfortable or decides to leave. I really hope he'll relax and stay seated by me.

But then my phone rings loudly, causing him to fly off the couch with his fur standing on end. He rushes back to his crate and curls up in the back corner of it. I sigh. Of course, whoever is calling me couldn't have known this was a bad time, but it still leaves me frustrated. That was the closest Tyson had ever gotten to me on his terms.

I glance at my ringing phone. It's my mom. Makes sense. She's one of the only people who calls me randomly without texting first. I've reminded her that I don't like unexpected phone calls, but she doesn't seem to understand.

I pick up the phone. "Hi, Mom. Tyson was finally close to me and your phone call scared him. I hope this is important." I chuckle as I speak so she knows I'm partially joking.

She doesn't laugh back. "Why didn't you tell me about your soulmate?"

I flinch at the unexpected volume of her voice. She sounds furious. I can't remember the last time I've heard my mom raise her voice at me. My face turns bright red. "What are you talking about?"

"I felt so bad that you hadn't gotten your SoulSearcher yet, so I called the SoulSearcher Help Center to see what the issue was. They told me you already received it."

"Huh? Why would they give you that information?"

"That's not important. Why have you been lying to me? They said you received it over a month ago. We don't lie to each other, Rory."

She's right. For the most part, we have a pretty open and honest relationship, but soulmates are the one thing I'm not honest about. Yet, she doesn't know that. I'm so tempted to tell another lie to get out of this conversation, but I can't bring myself to do it. My mom is important to me, and I want her to know the truth.

"Okay, you're right. I was technically matched with a soulmate." I take a deep breath. "But I don't want a relationship like that, so she's my friend and that's it."

"She? Did they accidentally match you with a girl? You can get that fixed, sweetie. Don't worry."

"No, that's what I'm trying to say. There's nothing to fix."

"But you're not a lesbian."

I clench my fist. "Wait, would it be bad if I was?"

There's a pause on the other line. Somehow, this topic has never come up between me and my mom. What if she's homophobic? I'm sure she's not, but I'd have a hard time feeling comfortable around her from now on if that's the case.

"No, of course not," she says finally. "I just really hoped you would've told me by now." Another pause. "Is that what you're trying to tell me?"

I breathe a sigh of relief. "No, I'm not a lesbian. But I'm not straight either. I don't want a romantic relationship at all, so that's why it didn't work out with the person I got matched with."

"What do you mean you don't want a romantic relationship?"

My heart races, but I spit the words out before I can overthink it. "I'm asexual and aromantic. So, I don't feel sexual or romantic attraction toward anyone."

"Oh," she says softly. "Rory, it's okay to be picky. You'll find the right person one day."

"No, I won't. And I don't want to. I don't feel attraction to anyone and I've decided that a relationship isn't for me. I'm happy with who I am. I just wanted to let you know the real me."

"Okay." There's a long pause, but that's to be expected. I'm sure this is the last conversation she expected to have when she called me. "Then why would you even sign up for a SoulSearcher in the first place?"

"Because you always made me feel like I had to. You never stopped talking about how great it was, and whenever I tried to tell you I wasn't interested in it, you ignored me."

Silence. At first, I wonder if she's still there, but then she sighs. "Oh. That was never my intention. You know that, right?"

"I know. But that didn't make it hurt any less."

"Wow. You're right, maybe I have been a little pushy. But the SoulSearcher was so magical for me and your step-dad. I just wanted you to experience the same joy in life as me."

"I appreciate it, but that's not what's going to bring me joy. I find joy in helping animals and baking delicious desserts, not by falling in love."

"Are you sure? Falling in love is one of the greatest feelings in the world."

"I'm sure."

"Okay."

We're both silent for a moment, and I have no idea how she's handling it. I know her initial reaction wasn't perfect, but it seems like she's trying to understand. And it's clear that she loves me.

"Mom, I know it's a lot of information to take in, but I'm glad I finally told you."

"I'm glad you told me too. But I think it'll take me a while to process it. A life without romance just sounds so lonely."

"Take all the time you need to wrap your head around it."

"Thank you for being honest with me. I'm sorry you felt like you couldn't before." She sniffles, which makes my heart sink. I don't want her to cry because of me. "I love you so much, Rory. No matter what you do in life."

Now I'm the one tearing up. "I love you too, Mom."

I hang up and flop back on my couch. I want to smile and sob all at the same time. But in a good way. It's like a weight has lifted off my shoulders. I know my mom doesn't understand me completely, but that's okay. The important part is that she's really trying.

To make the situation even better, Tyson hops back on the couch. As if he's comforting me from a distance.

Chapter Twenty
Mila

When I return to my apartment the next morning, Kiki tackles me and showers me with kisses. I wrap my arms around her and squeal with delight. Last night with Aero had been one of the only nights I'd been apart from my dog in years. Even though it had been just over 12 hours, it felt like weeks.

"Oh, Kiki, I missed you so much. I promise I'll never leave you alone for that long again. I hope Liz took good care of you."

As if on cue, my little sister storms out of her bedroom. She scowls. "Mila, where were you?"

"What do you mean? I texted you."

"Hm, well let's look at the text you sent me." She pulls her phone out of her pocket and squints at the screen. "It says, 'Met my soulmate. Be back in the morning. Please let Kiki outside before bed.'"

"Yeah, that pretty much sums it up. Thank you so much for letting Kiki out. I was worried about her."

"Apparently, you weren't worried enough to answer follow-up texts or come back home. And what do you mean you found your soulmate? You can't just send vague, life-changing texts like that and expect me to be okay with it."

She crosses her arms as she waits for me to explain. I sigh. "Look, I'm really sorry, but it would've been too hard to explain over text, so I figured I'd wait to tell you in person. My soulmate's name is Aero, we connected through a database of people who turned in their SoulSearchers, and we had an amazing date last night. Also, he's on his way here right now so you can meet him!"

"I'm sorry, what? You invited him here without even asking me?"

"Well, yeah. He's my soulmate, so he's welcome whenever. You always brought Sawyer here without running it by me first."

She maintains her stern gaze. "Sawyer didn't come here until over a month after I met him. And I always asked you until it became a routine. You've known this guy for what, like a week? He's basically a stranger to you, and he's a stranger to me."

Technically, I've only known him for about two days now, and only in-person for one day, but I don't see a point in correcting her. "Liz, can you please just give him a chance? I really like him and he's going to be a big part of my life. I really want the two of you to get along."

On that note, her face softens. "Yeah, you're right. I'm sorry. Of course, I want to get along with him, especially if he makes you happy. I just wish you would've talked to me about it before jumping into this whole thing. I hate how our communication has been off lately."

I nod. "Me too, and I'm sorry. I just got so excited about him that I didn't think to talk to anyone first. I promise that from now on, I'll keep you updated."

"Thanks," Liz says. She smiles and her eyes water slightly, so I lean in and give her a big hug. She hugs me back tightly, and it brings back so many memories. I've missed hugging my sister like this. I've missed feeling close to her.

But then, our heartfelt moment is interrupted by a knock on the door. He's here! My soulmate is here and he's about to meet the other most important person in my life. Not only that, but he gets to meet Kiki. I hope Kiki loves him as much as I do. I let go of Liz and rush to the door.

"That's probably him," I say. "Promise me you'll get to know him before making any judgements?"

She nods. "Of course. Now, let him in so I can meet this mystery man."

Without hesitation, I open the door, and there's Aero standing on the other side. He grins and rushes into the apartment to kiss me. I hope our physical chemistry doesn't make it obvious what we ended up doing last night. My sister doesn't need to know about my sex life.

But the second our lips meet, Kiki leaps forward and shoves her way between us. Her tail flops back and forth like crazy as she sniffs Aero thoroughly.

I'd always expected my soulmate to love Kiki just as much as they love me, but Aero's first instinct is to jump backwards. His eyes are wide with fear. I try not to take it personally. The media doesn't paint dogs like Kiki in a very good light, so many people are cautious at first. But anyone who has gotten to know my dog can confirm that she's a teddy bear.

Kiki must sense his discomfort because she doesn't try to follow him. Instead, she backs up and sits beside me. I scratch her behind the ear and tell her she's a good girl.

"Is that your dog? You have a Pit Bull?" The way he says it makes it sound like he's accusing me of a crime.

"Um, yeah. This is Kiki, the dog I talked about at dinner. Her photo was on my profile. And yes, she's a mutt, but she definitely has some Pittie in her. That doesn't define her though. I promise she's very well-trained and super lovable. You two are going to become great friends!"

My words don't make him less tense. He stays as close to the front door as possible. If he wasn't blinking, you might mistake him for a statue. "Everyone says that until their Pit Bull bites someone." It feels like he's stabbing my heart as he says it.

I hold my breath, trying so hard not to say what I really feel. I want to tell him how skewed the media is. How "Pit Bull" is such a loose term and people will use it on any dog that slightly looks like a Pit Bull, even if the DNA says otherwise. How people are less likely to report a bite if it's from a "friendlier" breed. I could go on and on, but if I went into one of my dog lectures, would Aero still like me? I don't want to risk it.

"Well, Kiki is my dog. She's my best friend. So, please, get to know her so you can see her the way that I see her. If I was worried she would bite you, I would've put her in the other room immediately, but I know my dog's body language and she's as happy as can be," I say. It still comes out a little more lecture-like than I want, but it's definitely the watered-down version of my true feelings.

He looks into my eyes and then lets his muscles relax for the first time since he looked at Kiki. He glances down at her, and she wags her tail when she realizes she's being acknowledged. "Okay, fine. I'm sorry, but I'd like to keep my distance from her until I feel more comfortable."

"Of course." I say, even though his behavior so far is frustrating. I never considered that he'd have a problem with my beloved dog.

"Hi, I'm Liz," my sister speaks up, causing my face to turn bright red. I forgot that she was there, and I'm sure that conversation was not the best first impression of Aero. But Liz doesn't look upset. If she is, she's hiding it very well. She extends her hand toward Aero to shake.

Aero looks relieved to not be focusing on Kiki anymore because he quickly takes my sister's hand and shakes it. "I'm Aero. It's nice to meet you."

"Why don't we hang out in the living room where it's more comfortable?" I suggest. "Please, make yourself at home, Aero. Do you want anything to drink?"

"Water would be great, Babe."

Babe? I notice Liz smirk slightly at the pet name, but I think it's pretty cute. No one has ever called me Babe before.

I motion for Kiki to follow me into the kitchen as I blush the whole way there. Even as I pour a glass of water for my boyfriend, I can't stop smiling. I guess this is what love feels like: getting excited over every little thing. Even just calling him "boyfriend" in my head makes my heart race.

I bring the glass into the living room and gently set it on the coffee table in front of Aero. He and Liz are talking about his job, and they both seem at ease around each other. Definitely a good sign!

I sit on the couch beside him, so close that my skin brushes up against his. I motion for Kiki to sit next to me, hoping Aero won't mind since I'm in between the two of them.

"So, what made you turn in your SoulSearcher?" Liz, who's sitting on the chair across from us, asks suddenly.

"Wow, you and Mila sure like to get straight to the point," he says with a chuckle.

"Oh, well, I'm glad she asked you. It's important to know." Her words are serious, but she's still smiling innocently.

He takes a sip of his water before explaining. "I was matched with someone, but we weren't compatible. The details are pretty personal, so I'd rather not share too much. But you know how it is, SoulSearchers aren't always accurate. What Mila and I have is much stronger than anything I experienced in my last relationship." I can't help but wonder what the personal details are.

"That makes sense. I understand," Liz says. "I've also had some troubles with my SoulSearcher recently and I'm wondering if I should return it."

"Wait, really?" I ask. "I know you said you're not interested in Sawyer anymore, but I didn't think you'd want to find a soulmate the old-fashioned way like me."

"I'm not. In fact, I'm the opposite of you. Instead of rushing to find a soulmate, I'd like to take a break from it all and focus on myself for now. I don't need to date around or have a SoulSearcher."

"Why wouldn't you want a soulmate?" I ask.

Suddenly, Liz shakes off her polite act. "Seriously? After spending all that time with Rory, you still don't understand that romance isn't a priority for everyone?"

My cheeks grow hot at the mention of Rory. I hadn't said her name to Aero and I hadn't even told him that I was attracted to women too. It didn't seem important to mention yet, but now, I'm wondering if he'll judge me for it.

"You're right, I'm sorry," I say. "But please don't make it sound like Aero and I moving quickly is a bad thing. This is the happiest I've ever been. And if we're meant to be, then why take it slow?"

I reach over and take Aero's hand. He laces his fingers with mine. I can tell that Liz is itching to say how she really feels because she has the same crazy look that I likely had when I was trying not to go on and on about Pit Bulls before.

But like me, Liz is good at choosing when she speaks her mind. She takes a deep breath to compose herself and then resumes the conversation as if her brain didn't just flood with things to say. "You're right. You're both adults, you can do whatever. But when you say you're not taking it slow, what exactly does that mean? You're not getting married already, are you?"

Are we? I didn't think so, but I wouldn't be opposed to the idea. "Well, right now, we're boyfriend and girlfriend. That's about all we've established so far," I say.

"But I'd love for us to move in together whenever Mila is ready," Aero chimes in.

"You would?" I glance at him, my eyes watering slightly. He just met me yesterday, and he already thinks I'm great enough to live with? How sweet!

"Of course. You're my soulmate! And your apartment is so small and cluttered. Plus, I'm sure it's difficult for you to pay the rent with your dog jobs, so move in with me. If you want," he says. "I have lots of space and I'd love to have you by my side all the time."

His condo *is* extremely nice. But last night, I didn't really get to experience it much. He never gave me the tour he promised because we spent most of our time in his bed. It had been really weird and honestly, it didn't live up to the hype. I certainly don't want to have to do that every night, but maybe it would get more fun once I actually know what I'm doing.

"Yeah, I'd love to live with you. But I can't leave Liz alone with the rent."

I glance at Liz to gauge her expression. Her eyebrows are furrowed while she bites her lip, but she doesn't speak up. Ever since Liz was old enough to move out of our dad's house, the two of us have shared a place. Not living with Liz would be such a drastic change for me and my sister. But I knew this would have to happen at some point.

"My condo is already paid for, and you don't have to worry about bills. I'll keep handling that. So, if you want to live with me and keep paying rent here until your sister finds a roommate, that would be fine with me," Aero says.

"Oh, wow. Thank you. But would you be okay with Kiki living at your place?"

He glances at my adorable hippo-like dog as if he'd forgotten about her. She flops onto her back and wags her tail rapidly. I can't leave her hanging, so I give her a belly rub, which makes her tail move even faster until it's a blur.

"Well, I think my neighborhood might have some breed restrictions."

I roll my eyes. Breed restrictions are the stupidest things. If they were really worried about aggressive dogs, they would want to meet the dogs in person or have them take a temperament test rather than just saying yes or no based on breeds. But I'm sure Aero doesn't want to hear about all that. "Her adoption paperwork lists her as a 'terrier mix,' so there's no proof that she has a restricted breed in her. I've never done a DNA test."

"Why wouldn't you get a DNA test? Don't you want to know what kind of dog you have so you don't need to lie on her paperwork?"

"I don't care what kind of dog she is. She's my dog and I love her, so that's all that matters to me. Besides, it's not lying. She likely has some terrier in her, such as an American Pit Bull Terrier or Staffordshire Bull Terrier..."

He opens his mouth to argue further, but then he stops himself and examines me snuggling with my pup. He sighs, as if he has finally realized that there's no way to separate me from Kiki.

"Okay, I guess you're right. She's your dog, so obviously, she can come with you."

"Thank you!" I let go of Kiki for a second to give Aero a huge hug. Kiki wags her tail as if she wants to celebrate with us, but she clearly has no idea what we're celebrating. "But as we're moving my stuff over, we need to take some time to help you get to know Kiki better. I want both of you to feel comfortable around each other before we make this big step."

"Or," Liz chimes in, "you could wait to move in together so you can make sure Aero and Kiki get along first. It would give the two of you time to get to know each other better as well."

My face gets hot. Liz's opinion makes sense, but I don't want to wait. I want to be around Aero all the time.

"Are you not supportive of our relationship?" Aero asks.

"I never said that. Again, you're both adults who can make your own decisions. But rushing into a relationship doesn't make it stronger. If anything, it hurts it by forcing things to happen before you're both ready. I'm just looking out for you."

"Well, I'm ready for this step and it seems like Mila is too. And, no offense, but I don't think she needs dating advice from her little sister," Aero says.

"Maybe not, but I want to hear Mila say she's ready for it. I don't like that you're speaking for her."

Is he speaking for me? Or is this something I really want? I glance back and forth between the two of them a few times before speaking up. They're both staring at me, eagerly waiting for my input. Even Kiki perks her ears up as if to ask, 'what's your decision?' And everyone knows I can't ignore Kiki.

"He's right," I say confidently. "I really want to move in with him. I'm ready."

Chapter Twenty-One
Rory

It has been about two weeks since I've seen Mila. I thought she would have reached out by now to apologize or at least see how I'm doing, but my phone has been silent. Even though Liz told me Mila was safe the day after the party, I can't help but worry. But I can't bring myself to call Mila either. I want to respect her space.

I'm not doing a very good job with that because, here I am, standing in front of her apartment door. It's not because I'm creepy or anything. Liz asked me to. She didn't explain why, but I jumped at the opportunity to see Mila and hopefully save our friendship. My body shakes, but I try my best to shove my worries aside.

Before I can overthink it, I ring the doorbell.

I hear shuffling coming from inside before Liz yanks the door open. "Rory! Come in, please."

"Is everything okay?" I ask as I enter the apartment.

Liz sighs. "No, not really. I'm relieved to see you because I need someone to talk about Mila with. Things have gotten way out of hand and no one seems to understand why I'm bothered by it."

That's when I notice that the apartment is a little emptier than before. A lot of the dog posters that were on the wall are missing. Also, Kiki isn't there to greet me. "Is Mila home?"

"Mila moved out."

"Wait, what?"

"A few days ago, she packed up all her things and moved in with her new soulmate." She scrunches up her face as she speaks, as if she's eating sour candy. "Ugh, I hate calling him her soulmate."

"Huh?" There's a lot of information to process in those few sentences, but before I can stop myself, I rush over to Mila's room and look in. Her bed is still there, neatly made, along with her dresser and nightstand, but everything else is gone. There's no hint that Mila and Kiki ever lived here, except for the occasional dog hairs floating around.

"It's okay. Take some time to process if you need," Liz says as she enters Mila's former room and sits on the edge of the bed. I sit beside her, but my brain floods with a million thoughts.

"So, you're saying that in only two weeks, Mila met a soulmate, started an official relationship with them, and moved in with them. How is that even possible?" I ask. "That's something that would happen in a really old fairy tale, not real life."

"Trust me, I'm just as baffled as you are. That's why I'm so glad to see you. For some reason, our dad isn't worried. He asked her if she was sure this was what she wanted a few times. Now, he's just happy that Mila's happy, even though he hasn't met the guy yet! Maybe he's right and I should just be happy for her, but I can't stop worrying."

"I know it's ridiculously fast, but Mila was set on falling in love, so I guess it makes sense for her. Is there a specific reason you're so worried?"

She nods. "Yeah, he gives me bad vibes. He doesn't seem to like dogs much. That alone should be a deal-breaker for Mila. And he seems to look down on her because he gets paid way more than her. I don't know, maybe I'm crazy, but something seems off about him. He just doesn't feel genuine. My instincts are normally pretty good."

I try my best to keep a neutral face since I've never met him, but now I'm worried. "Yeah, those aren't great signs. What else do you know about him?"

"Well, his name is Aero. I guess his situation was similar to hers; he was matched with someone he wasn't compatible with. So, he hit it off with Mila, and since they're both hopeless romantics, they had no problem rushing into things."

"Wow," I say. Because, really, what else can I say? But then, I hesitate as a peculiar thought pops in my head. "Wait, his name is Aero? Why does that sound so familiar?"

"Do you know him?" Liz sits up straighter and stares at me.

I shake my head. "No, I don't think so, but I'm sure I've heard that name before. It's not a name you hear every day."

Liz chuckles. "Yeah, it sounds like a name out of a fantasy movie."

I let out a faint laugh, but I'm too busy focusing on where I've heard the name before to respond. I swear someone mentioned Aero recently, and I don't think it was in a positive way. Was it a fellow volunteer? A coworker?

Suddenly, it comes to me. "Oh! My friend Zaya. She said her former soulmate was named Aero."

"Really? It must be him, right? How many Aeros can there be around here?"

I shrug. "I don't know what he looks like, but she didn't have good things to say about him. I hope it's not the same guy."

"Well, considering what I know about him so far, it's possible. What did she say?"

I blush, not sure if I want to go into details. I know I'm not supposed to share what's discussed in the support group without consent. "Basically, he was just really pushy about sex. I don't know if she'd be comfortable with me sharing more details than that."

"Oh. I really hope it's not the same Aero. I love Mila like crazy, but I imagine she'd have a hard time saying no to a soulmate, no matter how uncomfortable she was."

"Yeah, that's what I'm worried about too. But we shouldn't get too worked up until we know all the facts."

"Why don't you ask your friend Zaya for a picture of him? I've seen Mila's Aero, so I'll know if it's the same person."

I shake my head. "No, I can't do that to her. She obviously has a lot of bad memories from that relationship, so I don't want her to have to think about him."

Liz nods, but glances at the floor in defeat. "Yeah, that's understandable."

I pick up my phone and search Zaya's name on social media. "Unless..."

Liz leans over my shoulder as I scroll through some old photos on Zaya's social media account. Of course, there's no trace of any partner besides her current one. If she ever had any photos of Aero, they're long gone, which definitely confirms that she doesn't want reminders of him. I don't blame her.

I'm about to exit the app when Liz gently grabs my arm. "Wait," she says. "Can you click on that group photo?"

She points to a photo, so I click on it and zoom in. It's a picture of Zaya at an amusement park with a group of friends. As I examine the photo closer, it appears that they're all couples. And the guy who has his arm around Zaya is someone I've never seen before.

"That's him! It has to be," Liz says, pointing to the mysterious man. "He looks a lot like the Aero I met."

I tap on the photo, causing it to display everyone who's tagged in it. It looks like one of Zaya's friends posted it and tagged everyone, so that's why Zaya hadn't deleted it. Sure enough, the tag that appears next to the guy's face says, "Aero Ferguson." I hold my breath as I click on his account.

It only takes a second for me to discover that this is definitely the same Aero that Mila's dating. His profile photo shows him and Mila at the beach. Her arms are around him and she's grinning from ear to ear. She seems happy, but this situation doesn't sit right with me.

"Well, now we know it's him." Liz's voice is soft.

"Yeah, but he was with Zaya a few years ago, so maybe he has grown a lot since then." Am I trying to reassure her or myself? Probably both, but I don't believe a word coming out of my mouth.

"I doubt it. After all, he had a few red flags when I met him. Even though they were nothing crazy, they were probably just the tip of the iceberg," Liz says. "And Mila is head over heels for him, so she just lets all his questionable comments slide. Even when they're about something she's passionate about like Pit Bulls."

"Ugh, he didn't like Kiki?" I ask. Liz shakes her head. "But she's one of the sweetest dogs I've ever met. And I've met *a lot* of dogs."

"I know! If he does little things like that when meeting new people, then who knows how much worse he is behind closed doors?"

I try not to imagine it, but my mind wanders. I picture him giving her flowers and telling her how beautiful she is in public, but then leaving her crying whenever she's not perfect at home. But I hope I'm just exaggerating.

"You should warn her," Liz says.

"Me? She hasn't talked to me since the party. I'm sure she wouldn't listen to anything I have to say."

"Then I'll come with you. I know her new address, so we'll just show up, and she'll have to listen to both of us. Even if Aero is a better person now, I think it's important for her to know the truth. She can decide what to do with that information on her own."

I nod, but the idea of showing up unannounced at Mila and her sketchy partner's place sounds like a nightmare. Mila is still my friend though, even if she doesn't see me as a friend anymore. I just want to do what's best for her.

When I can't come up with a good reason to say no, I heave a sigh. "You're right. I think she needs to know." I know doing this will probably upset Mila more, but at least I'll leave this chapter of my life knowing I did the right thing.

"Good, let's go now," Liz says.

I want to tell her to take a beat to think over what we're going to say, but she's already heading out the door.

Chapter Twenty-Two
Mila

As I walk Kiki around my new neighborhood, I get lots of glares from people who then immediately cross the street. I'm sure someone in this fancy neighborhood is going to complain about my "terrifying Pit Bull," but I'm ready to fight back. Kiki hasn't done any harm.

Despite the judging looks, Kiki is oblivious, as always. She trots along the sidewalk happily, stopping to sniff every tree we pass. She doesn't even glance at the Doodles who bark at her like crazy. I'm glad my sweet dog doesn't have to waste her time worrying about what others think of her.

When I turn the corner, my phone rings, so I pull it out of my pocket. I'm so glad the dress I'm wearing has pockets! It makes walking Kiki much easier.

My phone reads 'front gate' as the contact name. "Hello?" I say as I lift my phone to my ear. Having to give people permission to enter the neighborhood is so weird, but it kind of makes me feel like royalty.

"Hi, Mila. This is Justin from the front gate. A woman in a white Volkswagen Beetle is here to visit you. She says she's your sister, Liz. Should I let her enter?"

It's unusual that Liz wouldn't have texted me before stopping by, but that's definitely the correct description of her car. Maybe she just misses me so much that she wanted to surprise me. "Yes, you can let her in. Tell her that I'm walking my dog, so she'll see me to her right once she drives through the gate."

"Okay, I'll let her know. Have a wonderful day, Mila."

"You too," I say as I hang up. A few seconds later, my sister's adorable little car enters the neighborhood. I wave to her. She helped me move stuff in, but other than that, she hasn't visited. I can tell she's still wary of the whole situation, claiming I'm moving too fast. I'm sure she'd feel better if she got to know Aero.

Liz sees me and pulls her car into a parking spot in front of me. Once the car is close enough, I realize that she's not alone. There, sitting in the passenger seat, is Rory. My blood runs cold as I rush to the driver's side of the car.

Even before Liz fully steps out, I aggressively whisper at her. "What is Rory doing here? Why would you bring her here without telling me?"

Rory gets out of the car too but keeps her distance. She likely heard what I said to Liz, but I don't care. Liz had no right to blindside me like this.

"Mila, please calm down," Liz says as she closes the car door. "We just have something to tell you, and we thought it'd be best if you heard it from both of us."

I narrow my eyes at Liz, then at Rory. Despite standing closer to Liz, Kiki pulls herself toward Rory with her tail wagging. I motion for her to sit beside me, and she does reluctantly.

When I meet Rory's gaze, my heart skips a beat. There's no doubt that I still have feelings for her, which is exactly why I don't want to see her. I feel more comfortable around her than I do with Aero. But she doesn't want me, Aero does. She's not my soulmate, Aero is. Part of me wonders if she's here to finally confess her love for me, but I know that's not realistic.

I turn back to Liz. "Wait, have you been hanging out with her behind my back? You two were never friends before."

"No, this is the first time we've seen each other since the party," Liz says. "But why does it even matter?"

"There's a reason I haven't contacted you," I say to Rory. "I need to distance myself from you so I can get over you. And besides, I'm happy now with Aero. I don't want you being in my life to mess that up." Shoot. Did I just admit that I still have feelings for Rory despite being in a relationship with someone else? I'm certain Aero wouldn't be happy about that.

"I understand, but I really need to tell you something. Then, I'll be out of your life, and you can reach out to me if you ever want to be friends again," Rory says. "Because I'd love to stay friends with you if you ever want that."

I feel my eyes water slightly, but I blink repeatedly to force the tears away. "I don't know if I'll want that. Please just say what you need to say so I can go back to my soulmate."

"Okay. It's about your soulmate, actually," she says. At first, I'm skeptical. I figure she must just be jealous that I've found someone new so quickly, but then she explains that Aero used to be matched with her friend, Zaya. She tells me about how Zaya felt pressured into sexual acts often, and Rory wants to make sure I don't ever feel that way. She even shows me a photo of Zaya and Aero together to prove it.

Once she's done talking, I have no idea what to say. I really wish I could say that everything she's telling me is ridiculous. That Zaya must've exaggerated it or that Aero has grown a lot since then. But honestly, I can imagine him being pushy about sex. I'd be lying if I said the thought hadn't crossed my mind. After all, he convinced me to do it for the first time when I told him I wasn't ready. And now that we've done it a few times, I still haven't enjoyed it. Yet, he always talks me into it and makes it sound like it will be incredible.

But I always consented, didn't I? I might've said no at first, but I always changed my answer to yes before he proceeded. So, it can't be as bad as they're making it sound. Right? Were they telling me this just to get in my head and make me question the man I love?

"I appreciate you telling me," I say when I realize I've been silent for too long. "But I love Aero and he makes me happy. So, even if he was a bad soulmate in the past, he's not bad for me."

"I'm really glad to hear that," Rory says. "We thought you deserved to at least know the truth."

I can't help but wonder why Aero hasn't told me much about his past, especially if things were so serious with his ex. But I shake my head, brushing my worries away.

"Mila, we care about you and just want what's best for you," Liz says.

I glance back and forth between them. "Then give me some space for now. I trust Aero, so I'm going to spend more time with him."

I motion for Kiki to follow me as I walk back toward Aero's, I mean our, condo. Kiki resists slightly because she still wants to say hi to Rory, but I don't let her. I can't let Rory and Liz know how much I miss them. The only way they'll trust Aero is if I paint him to be as perfect as possible. Besides, he cares about me, so that's the most perfect trait he could have.

When I enter our home, I hear him get up and approach me as if he had been waiting for the doorknob to turn. Kiki wags her tail, but he brushes past her to hug me. "Mila, where have you been?"

"Um, I was just walking Kiki like I told you."

"I know, but your walks don't usually last that long. Did something happen?"

I'm pretty sure I was only gone about ten minutes longer than usual. It's a bit odd that he's been keeping track of my walks that closely. For a few moments, I wrestle with whether or not I should tell him. But a relationship filled with lies is doomed, right? And lying has caused me nothing but trouble lately.

"Liz and Rory stopped by to say hi. It was a surprise to me, I promise."

Aero crosses his arms. "Isn't Rory your former soulmate? I thought you stopped talking to her."

"Well, technically, she was never more than a friend to me, and she wants to stay friends."

"Are you going to? I thought she broke your heart?"

"I'm not sure. And she did, but not on purpose. She was honest with me the whole time." As I say it, I finally hear the truth. Why have I been so mad at Rory? She made it very clear that she never wanted to be more than friends. I'm the one who couldn't accept that.

"I would stay away from her if I were you. She sounds like trouble. And from now on, let me know if something comes up like this. I was worried about where you were."

"Okay, I will." As soon as I say it, the stern gaze disappears from his face and he wraps his arms around me. I hug him back, but I don't feel the way I'd always imagined I'd feel when hugging my soulmate. Instead of feeling warm and safe, I feel nothing.

Chapter Twenty-Three
Rory

As I organize the snack table, my heart races. In less than a half hour, the LGBTQ+ center will be full of people. Sure, it would be good to make some friends, but the thought of being near so many people at once overwhelms me. Especially since the last time I was around a large group of people was Mila's party.

"Thanks for helping me set up," Zaya says as she hangs up another rainbow banner.

"Of course," I say, even though I considered not coming several times. But I couldn't back out at the last minute. That would be extremely rude to Zaya.

Unfortunately, I feel more awkward than usual because I haven't told Zaya that Mila is dating her ex yet. I thought about it, but I wasn't sure how she would react. And telling her right before the big event she's been looking forward to seems harsh, so I guess it will have to wait until after everyone leaves.

"So, how many people usually come to events like this?" I ask.

"A lot! I bet all these tables will be full. It'll be the perfect place for you to make new friends. Hanging out with other people in the community really helped me while I was figuring out my sexuality."

"I've got my sexuality figured out, but I am nervous about meeting so many strangers."

"Mila was a stranger, but you seemed to bond with her quickly."

"Yeah, but she approached me. And right away, I knew she was a dog person, so there was something easy to talk about."

"Then ask people about their pets tonight. Lots of people love animals, so I'm sure you'll find someone who will talk about it with you."

She's right. Most people have at least one pet, so it's not a bad conversation starter. But if they don't, how do I change the subject? Or leave the conversation? And even if they do love animals, what if they don't love them in the same way I do? I can't connect with someone who buys "designer" dogs instead of rescuing. I sigh. "Yeah, I'm just overthinking it."

She walks to the snack table, where I've reorganized the platters several times. They never look just right. She gently slides the platter of rainbow cupcakes toward me. "Would a cupcake boost your confidence?"

I smile. Even though I made the cupcakes, I never get sick of my baking. "Maybe later. I don't want to be the first one to take a snack."

"Rory, no one will care about that."

Of course, she's right. But she doesn't understand. She's so good around people. She knows how to make everyone instantly like her. She's like the cool big sister I never had.

I glance at a mirror on the wall and get a good look at myself. I'm wearing a purple dress that's surprisingly beautiful on me. Dresses aren't normally my style, but I figured I should make more of an effort tonight. Plus, purple is one of the colors of the asexual flag, so it seemed fitting. I smile at my reflection for a moment. Even if I don't feel confident, at least I look like I could be.

Zaya and I do a bit more organizing before people flow through the front door. Many of them are decked out in their pride attire, making me feel a little guilty for not having any rainbow accessories of my own. All of them have wide smiles like Zaya, and they head right to the food table. Once a few people have grabbed cupcakes, I decide it's acceptable for me to take one too.

After I've obtained a cupcake, I sit at a table beside Zaya, who's already in the middle of a conversation with someone else. I plan to just sit there quietly with my cupcake, but once Zaya notices I'm there, her face lights up.

"Rory, we were just talking about you! This is Elijah, and he has a dog. I bet you two would get along well."

Before I can say another word, she leaves, forcing me to sit across from a stranger. I glance up at Elijah, mortified. But he seems friendly. He has messy dark hair with a bisexual flag bandana on his head. He laughs, and his friendly expression clears some of the awkwardness. "Sorry about that. Zaya is quite the character," he says.

My body relaxes slightly. "Yeah, tell me about it. She's determined to help me make some friends today. If you couldn't already tell, I suck at it."

"I can't tell. You seem cool."

I seem cool? What am I supposed to say to that? I hate when people don't try to continue the conversation. But for all I know, Elijah could be just as nervous as me. I need to channel my inner Zaya.

"So, what's your dog like?" I ask.

His smile lets me know that my conversation starter was a success. "She's a Golden Retriever named Daisy. I've only had her for a few months, but she's such a silly girl."

Part of me wants to ask where he got her from, but if he says a puppy store, then I might not be able to hide my disappointment. I always try to be understanding with people, but I don't think I could be friends with someone who supported a puppy mill. I force my body to relax. "Come on, you need to show me a picture!"

"Oh, of course. She's the only thing I've taken pictures of recently." He pulls out his phone and shows me his lockscreen, which is an adorable young Golden Retriever wearing a pink bandana. Her sweet puppy face melts my heart.

"My dog is my lockscreen too. This is my cute little mutt, Minnie." I turn on my phone to show him.

"She's adorable!" He glances at my phone for a second, but then goes back to scrolling on his phone to find another picture. I don't mean to look, but I quickly see that not all his pictures are of his dog because there's one shirtless selfie of him. Yuck. I look away and try my best not to cringe.

He holds up his phone so it's easier for me to see, and luckily, the screen now shows another photo of his beloved puppy. She's lying on her back playfully with a toy in her mouth.

"I love that so much! I wish I could pet her," I say.

"Well, maybe we could take our dogs for a walk together some time. I think that's what dog-loving friends do, right?"

"Yeah, absolutely. Any activity where my dog can come is instantly better." I quickly think of something else to talk about before the conversation dies. "I also have a foster dog named Tyson. I'm not sure what breed he is, but he's the cutest."

I show Elijah a photo of Tyson on my phone. His eyes widen. "Wow, that's amazing that you foster. He looks super sweet. I'd adopt him in a heartbeat if my lease let me have a second dog."

"He is sweet, but in his own way. He's very timid and scared of people, so he spends a lot of time hiding in his crate. But he's really starting to come out of his shell."

Of course, Elijah proceeds to ask me about fostering and how I can possibly give up the dogs. It's what everyone wonders, so I've gotten pretty good at explaining it. I have endless stories and information about fostering. As long as the other person is still interested, I can talk about it forever.

I like talking to Elijah. I don't know if he'll become a life-long friend or anything, but he's probably someone that I could hang out with once in a while. To avoid sounding too self-centered, I decide to ask him more questions about himself. But before I can, my eyes catch a vibrant figure in the distance.

My eyes focus on the newcomer, and my jaw drops. I rub my eyes to make sure I'm not imagining things. Sure enough, Mila is here! She's wearing a frilly hot pink dress that definitely makes her stand out in a crowd. She looks around worriedly, but when she sees me, a smile forms.

"Hey, do you mind if I talk to that girl for a second? It's kind of important," I say to Elijah. I worry he'll be mad or disappointed, but he nods and smiles. Before I disappear, I give him my number in case we don't get another chance to talk. Then, I rush over to Mila.

Without thinking twice, I give her a friendly hug, and she hugs me back without hesitation. But then I pull away, in fear that she'll think it's something more than just an "I missed you, best friend" hug.

"Rory, don't worry. I didn't think that was a romantic hug or anything." She chuckles.

"I just want to be cautious. I never want to lead you on, and I'm really sorry if I accidentally did in the past."

"No, I'm the one who needs to be apologizing. You were very clear about your feelings from the beginning. I'm the one who kept holding out hope. If I were you, I'd be furious with me, but for some reason, you keep wanting to be my friend. And that means a lot to me."

"Wait, so you still want to be friends? You're not mad at me?"

"No, I'm not mad. I just want things to go back to the way they were."

I nod. "Then let's do that."

"Great," she says. "And I just want to say thank you for that hug. I know how much you hate physical contact, so I'm glad you feel comfortable around me, even after everything that went down."

Again, I nod and smile, but I'm not sure what else to say. Does "you're welcome" make sense? Not really.

After a moment of silence, I glance at the snack table. "Do you want any snacks? I can confirm that they're delicious."

"Well, if you made any of the desserts, I know those will be my favorite."

"Then you'll love the cupcakes."

Mila beams and rushes over to the snack table. She grabs a cupcake and then takes several desserts with chocolate. Once her plate is full, she leads me to a table. Luckily, I can see that Elijah has joined a new conversation, so I don't feel as guilty about ditching him anymore.

After sitting down, I clear my throat. "I can't believe you actually came. After our last interaction, I was sure you didn't remember or care that I invited you."

"I'm a little insulted that you think my memory is that bad," she jokes.

"You know what I mean." And just like that, it feels like nothing has changed between us. It's as if we never shared that awkward kiss and she never moved out of her apartment to be with a questionable soulmate.

But she did do that. And I don't want to ignore the elephant in the room.

"Look, I know that last time I saw you, I said some pretty serious things. But it was just because I thought you should know. It wasn't because I wanted to end your relationship or anything. If you're happy with Aero, then I'm happy for you. I promise."

Her smile wavers for a moment, but she forces it back into place. "Thanks, Rory. I appreciate your concern. I'm glad you told me, but Aero has grown a lot since his last relationship and he treats me well. I wouldn't have chosen him as my soulmate if he didn't."

Mila's body language definitely isn't agreeing with her words. She's having a hard time looking me in the eye, which is crazy because she normally has the best eye contact I've ever seen. But it isn't my place to call her out. If I want to be a good friend, I need to trust her.

"Okay, I'm happy to hear that. But if anything is ever wrong, in any aspect of your life, I want you to know that you can talk to me. I won't judge."

It seems like her eyes are almost watering, but maybe I'm imagining it. "Thank you, that means a lot."

"So, what do you think of this party? Pretty cool, right?"

She looks around at all the people gathered in brightly colored outfits and smiles. The worry in her eyes fades. "It's wonderful. I wish I would've checked out a Pride event sooner, but I just wasn't sure I belonged."

"Like I said before, everyone is welcome as long as they're kind."

"Well, even though I'm dating a man now, I know I'm not straight," she says. "Maybe I prefer men. I'm not sure. But I'm not only interested in men. I don't know if that even makes sense."

"It does. Of course, I can't relate since I'm the opposite: interested in no one. But I know there are a lot of people out there who feel the way you do."

She giggles, and it makes me feel at ease. If she's okay with me joking about my sexuality, then she must actually be okay with me not being interested in her romantically. It's a relief that we can finally move past that.

"Oh, let me show you a picture of this adorable dog that just showed up at the shelter," she says as she reaches into her purse for her phone. "Since we haven't talked in a while, you've missed out on a lot of cute dog content."

"Well, you better get me caught up then."

"Mila!" Before she pulls her phone out, a deep voice approaches. She freezes and her skin turns pale as a ghost. She doesn't do or say anything, as if she's hoping she can become invisible.

I look over her shoulder and see a man approaching her, looking furious. Right away, I recognize him from the photos on Zaya's social media. It's Aero.

"Mila, what are you doing here?" Aero says once he's close enough to put his hand on her shoulder. As soon as his fingers touch her skin, she flinches slightly and turns to him.

"Aero, why are you here? I told you I was going out," she says.

"You said you were going out with Liz, but then she stopped by to give you some of your stuff. She had no idea where you were, so of course, I was worried sick!"

"I'm sorry. I should've told you the truth, but I wasn't sure how you'd react. I'm fine though, so you can go back home."

I narrow my eyes at him. Even if Mila did lie, I don't like how harsh his tone is. "How did you even find her?" I ask, my voice shaking slightly.

For the first time, Aero glances at me. He looks me up and down and frowns. "Who the hell are you?"

I ignore his question. "Are you stalking her or something?"

"No, of course not. But I do have a location app so we can find each other in an emergency. It's what all couples should do."

Mila squirms in her seat for a moment, but she doesn't say a word. She's obviously uncomfortable with Aero being here. If he was truly a good match for her, she wouldn't be acting this way.

"Hold on. Are you Rory?" he asks. Then, he glares at Mila. "Is that why you didn't tell me? You wanted to sneak around with your little girlfriend?"

Surprisingly, Mila seems too scared to respond. So, I have no choice but to speak up. "Yes, I'm Rory. And I'm not her girlfriend. I've never been. I'm a friend who cares about her. Why wouldn't you want her hanging out with someone important to her?"

"Because you're a friend who broke her heart! And I don't want you trying to steal her from me."

I clench my fists and consider fighting back, but he's right. I did break Mila's heart, even though I didn't mean to. "Look, I promise I'm not interested in her like that. And if Mila still feels heartbroken, then I understand if she doesn't want to be friends with me. But you can't tell her who she can and can't hang out with." My whole body shakes as I raise my voice.

"I'm just looking out for her."

He's obviously full of shit. But Mila doesn't call him out on it. And if I get too harsh with him, it could hurt her more. I glance at Mila, waiting for her to tell us both what she really wants.

But she doesn't say a word. It's the longest I've heard her go without talking. Somehow, she looks smaller than usual as she sits quietly and stares down at her feet. A few minutes ago, she was laughing and smiling with me, but now, she's not acting like the Mila I know. No matter what she says, something is definitely wrong with this relationship.

When Mila doesn't speak up, Aero grabs her by the wrist and leans toward her. "Come on, Babe. Let's go home." He whispers it just loud enough for me to hear.

To my surprise, she nods slowly, grabs her purse, and stands up. She looks at me and mouths the word 'bye' before turning around and following Aero out the door. I want to chase them down and explain to both of them that this isn't okay. I want to make Mila see that she doesn't have to live like this. But is there anything I could say that would make a difference right now? Would she really rather be treated like this than be single?

I glance around the room, wondering if anyone else saw that weird exchange. Everyone is still chatting and enjoying some rainbow-colored snacks, not realizing that my friend could be in danger. I'm about to chase after Mila when I realize that someone else had noticed Aero's bizarre behaviors. It's the only person I wish hadn't.

Zaya stands across the room, frozen in place and pale like Mila had been. She's staring straight at the door Aero and Mila exited out of. She turns around and races in the opposite direction as quickly as she can, darting down a hallway far away from the crowd.

I speed walk after her. When I turn the corner, I see her sitting against the wall of a dark hallway all alone. Her knees are against her chest with her arms wrapped around them, which is an awkward position for someone wearing a dress. She's sobbing, causing her mascara to run slightly. If I hadn't seen her run this way, I wouldn't have recognized her at first. The Zaya sitting there isn't the bubbly, confident Zaya I've gotten to know. It's like how Mila's personality suddenly shrank when Aero appeared. Clearly, this guy is worse than I thought.

"Zaya? Are you okay?" I ask as I slowly approach her. I sit down beside her with my legs straight in front of me to keep my skirt in place. The darkness of this space is eerie, but it's hard to focus on anything besides Zaya. She's crying so much I can almost feel her pain.

She bats her eyelashes to let the tears escape her eyes. She doesn't even try to hide the fact that she was crying, which is what I would've done if I were in her situation. "That was Aero, wasn't it? I thought I was seeing things at first."

"Yeah, he's Mila's new soulmate," I say. "I recently found out and I'm really sorry I didn't tell you right away. I was planning to wait until after the event was over."

For some reason, I expect her to be furious with me for keeping this secret. But instead, she looks up at me with a defeated gaze. "Oh. What was he doing here?"

"Honestly, I don't know. He claimed he was just worried about where Mila was. I promise I didn't expect him to show up. I didn't even think Mila was coming!"

She reaches over and rests her hand on my shoulder. "Rory, it's okay. I'm not blaming you. Seeing him was just a lot for me. I'm really embarrassed that you have to see me react this way."

"Don't worry, I'm not judging you. I'm surprised to see you not your cheery self, but I know everyone has stuff they need to deal with."

She nods, moving her hand away from me. "Yeah, but I try so hard not to let that side of me show, especially since it's silly. Aero and I parted ways a long time ago, and I'm in a wonderful relationship now. I've moved on and I'm exactly where I want to be in life, but I guess that doesn't matter. Whenever I think about him too much or hear about him, it really brings me down. I think the pain that relationship caused me will always exist, and I hate it. I hate feeling weak."

I love that she trusts me enough to pour her heart out to me, but I really don't know what to say. I'm good at listening and being respectful, but when it comes to offering reassuring words, I always worry I'll mess it up.

Luckily, she keeps talking before I can say something stupid. "That was my first time seeing him in person since we broke up. If this is how I react just seeing him, then I can't even imagine what I'd do if he saw me or tried to talk to me."

I take a deep breath. "I'm sorry if this isn't appropriate to ask, but have you talked to anyone about these feelings before?"

She nods, but struggles to look me in the eye. "Of course. I've told Blake about it, and he's really good at comforting me. And I've talked with my therapist about it many times. But talking about it only makes it less painful. It doesn't fix the problem completely."

I feel horrible for her. There's no way for me to relate since I've never been in a relationship, let alone a bad one. But as I watch her sob in this dark hallway, I realize that this could be Mila in the future. Actually, Mila in the future could be in more pain than this if she doesn't get out of the relationship like Zaya did.

Zaya wipes her eyes and glances up at me. She seems to be studying my face, and somehow, that gives her a hint as to what's going on inside my head. "You must be really worried about Mila, right? You know, after seeing how much that guy hurt me."

"Well, yeah, but we don't have to talk about that if it's too hard for you."

"No, it's okay. I'm actually worried about her too even though I don't know her. I don't want anyone else to go through what I went through. It damaged me a lot mentally." She pauses for a moment, as if she's lost in thought. "But also, it has been a while since I've seen or spoken to Aero. What if he's a better person now? What if I'm spending all this time worrying for nothing?"

"That's what I kept telling myself, but I don't think that's the case. Something seemed off about Mila, and I didn't like the way he was talking to her. Even if he is a better person than when you knew him, I still don't think he's the right fit for Mila. But I don't know how long it'll take her to realize that on her own."

"Should we do something?"

I shake my head. "No, I already told her a little about your history with him. I hope that's okay." I pause to get her approval, and she nods. "I don't think there's much else I can do. It's up to her to come to her senses."

"But what if she doesn't? What if she stays with him longer than I did and his behavior just keeps getting worse?"

It's not something I want to think about, but it has crossed my mind. "Well, would you have listened if someone told you to break up with Aero back then?"

She considers it for a moment, but then shakes her head. "Nope. You're right. I was so desperate for love back then that I had convinced myself that was what true love was like. I ignored all the red flags because he was my 'soulmate.' I wouldn't listen to reason because I just assumed no one else knew what they were talking about. I was so naive."

"Yeah, that sounds like Mila's mindset now. She's a good person, but she's way too desperate to find love. I'm worried if I keep warning her about Aero, she'll just push me away."

Zaya nods and leans toward me, resting her head on my shoulder. I would prefer not to touch this much, but it seems to be comforting my friend. The tears in her eyes have subsided, but her face is still too red and puffy to return to the party. I have a feeling we'll be sitting here for a while.

I'm glad I can be here for Zaya, but seeing her like this is only making me worry about Mila even more. I really hope she comes to her senses soon.

Chapter Twenty-Four
Mila

I've found myself taking walks more often. During those walks, I've been able to interact with the few neighbors that aren't afraid of Kiki. Some of them have even shown interest in my dog training services. Aero doesn't like when I schedule too many training sessions, but lately, I feel like Kiki and my jobs are the only things keeping me sane.

As much as I love Aero, I'm starting to feel suffocated by him. Which is something I never thought I'd say. I feel horrible even thinking it, but it's true. He always likes to know where I am and what I'm doing. It's sweet that he cares so much, and I understand that he worries about me when I'm gone, but it's okay to have some alone time now and then. Most couples don't seem like they're attached at the hip like Aero wants to be.

Now, as I near our condo with Kiki, I wonder if I should take another lap. But if I do, Aero will definitely worry. He knows exactly how long it takes me to walk around this neighborhood, so even if I'm a minute or two off, he'll likely be mad.

"Excuse me! Are you the neighborhood dog trainer?"

I turn to see a blonde woman approaching with her fluffy dog. I tell Kiki to sit just in case this dog is out of control. The woman stops a few feet away, but her dog keeps trying to pull toward me.

"Yes, I'm a dog trainer. And I've been working with a few of the dogs around the neighborhood." I pause and look at her dog, who's struggling to sit still. "Are you looking for some training sessions?"

"No," she says immediately. "This is my perfect Bernedoodle, Finn. He doesn't need training. My neighbor pointed you out to me and said you were a wonderful trainer. But you're walking a *Pit Bull*, so what do you have to say for yourself?"

I frown and glance down at Kiki. My sweet dog is sitting patiently by my side, looking up at me instead of barking at the "perfect Bernedoodle." Finn is pulling on his leash and not focusing on his human at all.

"There's nothing to say. This is my dog, Kiki, and her breed isn't important. You can see that she's well-trained. I've had success training all kinds of dogs, no matter their breed."

"You *own* that dog?" she shrieks. "Why would anyone trust you with their dogs when you're walking around with a monster like that?"

Suddenly, I have a strong desire to scream or throw something at her, which isn't like me at all. But you can't mess with my dog, and I'm sick of snobby people thinking my dog is evil just because of her looks. This lady's "fancy" mutt is behaving much crazier right now than Kiki ever has.

"Because, like I said, it's not about the breed. All kinds of dogs can be trained with the right techniques." I take a deep breath to keep myself sane. "Now, if you're not going to ask about my services, then I'd really like to finish my walk alone."

I start to walk away, but as soon as I take a step, I hear her dog's nails scratching on the ground behind me, followed by her footsteps. "You can't live in this community with a Pit Bull! We have a long list of restricted breeds."

I stop walking and turn to face her. Again, I motion for Kiki to sit to prove to this woman that my dog is not a problem. The woman stops walking too, but her dog is uncomfortably close to me and Kiki.

"Yes, I'm aware," I say. "I think breed restrictions are awful, but even so, I'm not breaking the rules. Kiki's paperwork just says she's a 'terrier mix' and I'm not interested in paying for a DNA test, so the leasing office approved it."

"Well, I'm going to complain then."

I roll my eyes. Of course she is. Kiki is minding her own business while this crazy woman is speaking loud enough for anyone outside to hear. I should complain about her to the office.

I'm about to turn toward my door to avoid further interactions with her, but suddenly, Finn runs toward Kiki playfully. The woman has him on a retractable leash, so of course, it's impossible for her to pull him back.

Kiki wags her tail and leans forward to sniff him, but to my surprise, the woman screams and struggles to pull her dog back toward her with the flimsy leash.

"That Pit Bull attacked my dog!" she says loudly, even though no one else is around. My jaw drops. Kiki had slightly sniffed Finn while still sitting beside me. And even if she had growled or nipped, Finn was the one who approached her!

Suddenly, I don't feel confident. This is a serious accusation. Whether or not Kiki did anything will be irrelevant to many people. I know for certain Kiki and I behaved correctly, but since I have a Pit Bull-looking dog, I'm sure people will be hesitant to side with me if things escalate.

"Come on. We both know that my dog was just sitting here. What are you trying to pull?" I say, but my voice shakes slightly.

"I'm not trying to 'pull' anything. Your dog is a monster that tried to hurt my sweet baby."

"Stop spreading lies about my dog! My dog deserves love just like yours. Her appearance shouldn't matter. I know for a fact she's better behaved than your dog." I probably shouldn't be firing this woman up, but I can't hold it back any longer. Everything I've ever wanted to say to Pit Bull haters is coming up and I can't stop it.

Before this fight can continue, I hear a door slam shut behind me. I turn around to see Aero storming out of our home. Suddenly, I feel less angry. My soulmate must have heard I was in trouble and is coming to help me. I knew I was being too cynical about him before!

But instead of rushing over to the woman and telling her to leave me alone, he stops beside me and looks down at Kiki skeptically. "Mila, what's going on?"

"This woman is acting like Kiki did something bad, but all she's doing is sitting here."

He glances between me and the woman, who is still glaring at me intensely. Before he defends me, she starts shouting again about how Kiki attacked Finn. But Aero must know that she's being crazy, right? She sounds like an awful actress, and Aero has lived with Kiki long enough to know that she's not aggressive.

But instead of telling the lady she's full of shit, Aero just shakes his head. "I'm really sorry, ma'am. I'll handle it and make sure it never happens again."

He must be faking it, right? Just telling her what she wants to hear so she'll leave us alone? That's the only logical explanation I can think of. And if it is just an act, she believes it. She nods and thanks him.

Then, he grabs my arm and drags me back toward the condo before I can process what's happening. Kiki gallops behind me, still not paying attention to the crazy Doodle.

Once we're inside, I let Kiki off her leash, and I head over to the cabinet to grab her a treat. I hand her a dental stick, and she accepts it with a wagging tail. I giggle as she tosses it around the room. She deserves it after having to put up with that.

"What the hell are you doing?" Aero asks. "She just attacked a dog! She doesn't deserve a treat."

"Um, what are you talking about? She obviously didn't do anything to that dog. I thought you only said that to get the woman to leave us alone."

"If she didn't do anything, then why would that woman say she did?"

"Honestly, I don't know. But if I had to guess, it seems like she's out to get my dog just because she looks 'dangerous.' But come on, she's obviously not. Kiki barely acknowledged that dog."

He crosses his arms. "Mila, do you realize how crazy you sound?"

"Excuse me? That dog didn't have a single scratch. There was no attack!"

"Your dog is a Pit Bull. They're known for being dangerous, but you're constantly in denial about it."

"In denial? Not every dog of one breed is exactly the same," I say. "I work with dogs, and I've trained Kiki well. How can you still say all Pit Bulls are bad after living with Kiki for a while? She has never done anything wrong since she's been here."

"All the news sources say they attack unprovoked. Just because she hasn't bitten someone doesn't mean she won't."

"The news sources claim Pit Bulls have locking jaws too, which is scientifically incorrect. I can't believe you'd trust a random internet source more than your soulmate, who is around dogs every day!"

I feel guilty for raising my voice at him. I don't like to fight or escalate conflict. If Aero is mad, I usually just apologize or give him space to cool off. But this is a topic I can't ignore. People have been mean to my dog for no reason ever since I adopted her. I do not want my soulmate to be one of those people. I want him to love Kiki just as much as I do.

"Look, I didn't want it to have to come to this, but you need to get rid of that dog," he says.

At first, I'm not sure I heard him right. But what else could he have possibly said? Is he joking? Does he not understand how important Kiki is to me? "Excuse me? I'm not getting rid of Kiki. She's my baby, and she has been there for me way longer than you have."

"If you don't get rid of her, I'll report her for attacking the neighbor's dog."

"But she didn't attack the neighbor's dog! There's nothing to report." I don't want to look pathetic, but I can't stop myself from sobbing. I know Rory and Liz warned me about Aero, but I kept giving him the benefit of the doubt. Yet, there's no way to spin this situation to make him look like the good guy. Being mean to dogs, especially my dog, is a huge deal-breaker to me. I hate the word deal-breaker because it means I'm choosing to be single again, but Kiki is more important to me than anything. Even love.

"Well, that lady is a witness, so if I report it, I'll have one person to back it up," he says.

I can't believe the words that come out of my mouth, but there's nothing else to say. "Then, I guess we can't be soulmates. Kiki and I will get out of your hair so you don't have to deal with her anymore."

"Seriously? You're just going to give up on us that easily?"

"It's not easy at all. But you've put me in a position where I have no choice."

I pick up Kiki's leash, but before I can reattach it to her harness, Aero grabs me by my shoulders and pins me against the wall so I'm forced to stare straight into his eyes. He looks furious. He has never physically hurt me before on purpose. But now, I'm terrified that he's going to hit me, and I have no idea how to escape it.

"I will not let my soulmate choose a dog over me." He says the word 'dog' like it tastes bitter on his tongue.

Part of me wants to just agree with him so he'll let me go, but even when faced with danger, I can't betray my best friend. "Kiki is not just a dog to me. She's family, and I will never give her up."

"Oh yeah? What if I threaten to report the dog attack if you leave me? Then, will you stay with me to save Kiki's life? I've heard you blab about dogs enough to know that some Pit Bulls have been put down after one bite report."

My blood runs cold. Of all the dog tangents I've spouted, that's the one he actually paid attention to? He's right though. If he and the woman say Kiki bit her dog, there's a good chance I'll be forced to put her down. If she was a small dog or some Poodle mix, she'd likely get off with a warning. But sadly, our world isn't kind to certain dogs. Maybe I could save her by proving Finn doesn't have any bite marks, but is it worth the risk?

"Aero, you don't understand. Even if I for some reason agreed to give up Kiki, she likely still wouldn't survive. Shelters and rescues are so overcrowded, so if they're forced to euthanize dogs, the adult Pit Bulls will be the first to go." I'm not sure how much of that he understood through my tears, but I can't control myself. I always thought being without a soulmate was my worst fear, but this is worse than any nightmare my brain can come up with. Kiki being put down for a bite record is a terrifying, but so is her sitting alone in a shelter wondering why I abandoned her. I can't let either of those things happen.

He grips my arms tighter, causing me to wince in pain. "Then give her to a friend or something. I don't care. I just don't want to deal with her anymore."

I glance at Kiki, who has just finished her dental stick. When she sees me staring at her through pools of tears, she stands up and tilts her head. She lets out a little whimper as if to ask, 'what's wrong?'

"Come on, Mila. Just agree to it. If someone you trust takes Kiki, then she'll be safe and you'll still have a soulmate. It's a win-win for everyone." He leans closer to my ear. "But if you don't agree, your precious dog could die, and our relationship will likely be strained. We don't want that, do we?"

I need to say something quick. Every second we waste puts Kiki at a higher risk of being in danger. I can't bear to be apart from my dog, but I'd rather have her stay with someone else than any of the alternatives.

"Okay, fine. Can I please call someone to get Kiki's new living situation sorted out?"

Chapter Twenty-Five
Rory

"Hey, thanks for hanging out with me," Liz says as we sit at a table, ready to dig into the sandwiches we bought. "You're still the only person I can talk to about Mila. My dad still thinks I'm overreacting because I don't like living alone. I know he's just trying to be optimistic for Mila's sake, but I wish he'd listen." She sighs and shakes her head.

I nod as I take a bite of my sandwich. Right after the Pride event, I called Liz to tell her about the odd situation with Aero, and she grew just as concerned as I was. I hadn't told her about Zaya's meltdown because it didn't seem like something she would want me to share, but that had sent my worries over the edge. If anyone could help prevent Mila from meeting that same fate, it was Liz.

"You don't have to thank me. I'm glad we've become friends. Although, I wish the circumstances were better. As I've mentioned, making friends isn't my strong suit," I say.

"Well, didn't you meet some new people at that Pride event?"

"Sort of. I talked to this guy named Elijah who seemed pretty cool. And he has a dog, so maybe I'll hang out with him. But other than that, I didn't get the chance to connect with anyone else because I got caught up in all the Mila drama."

"I'm sorry to hear that. I'm really hoping all this stuff won't last long."

I consider straying away from the subject to lighten the mood, but Mila is one of the only things we have in common. And I know Liz doesn't have any pets, so there goes my only good conversation starter. "So, have you heard from her much lately?"

She nods. "Yeah, we talk regularly, but it's different. It's a lot of small talk and not much more. And of course, she never says many details about Aero because I'm sure he's in the room when she's talking on the phone. Even over text, she keeps her messages brief."

"Are you worried something's wrong?"

"I'm trying not to worry, but I know something is different. Not a good different. Although part of me wonders if Aero's history with your friend Zaya is preventing me from keeping an open mind."

"I thought the same thing, until I saw him in person. You were right, he didn't give off good vibes. But I don't know what to do."

She sighs. "Mila and I have always been there to support each other when needed, and now that I can't do that, I feel helpless."

Of course, I haven't known Mila my whole life like Liz has, but in a way, I understand. I'm about to keep talking about my worries, but then Liz's phone goes off, playing what sounds like a song from a TV show.

"Oh, speak of the devil," Liz says as she looks at her phone. "Do you mind if I take this?"

I shake my head. "No, not at all."

She gets up as she answers the phone and walks over to a corner of the restaurant where no one is sitting. I can't hear what she's saying, but I try to read her facial expressions. As I eat my sandwich, I feel like I'm snacking on popcorn while watching a drama movie. I feel bad for being so nosey.

I'm about to look away and scroll through my phone instead, but then I see Liz's face change from a casual talking expression to concern. And not just the slight concern you'd feel if someone fed your dog a little late, but closer to the fear that someone is dying.

As Liz looks more and more worried, I notice her raising her voice ever so slightly. Just loud enough where I can make out some words. I hear 'why,' and 'can't,' and most importantly, 'not okay.' But after what seems like an intense argument, she finally nods, and I can see her lips form the word 'alright.' Then, she slowly takes the phone away from her ear and hangs up. Her eyes linger on the screen for a few seconds. It looks like she's holding back tears.

Before she heads back toward the table, I glance at my phone and pretend like I've been looking at something this whole time. When I hear her chair pull out across from me, I glance up. Sure enough, her eyes are shiny as if she's on the verge of tears but refusing to let them out.

"Liz, what happened? Is something wrong?"

She shakes her head but refuses to cry. "Mila is giving me Kiki."

"What?" I must have misunderstood her. Mila would never give away Kiki. She and Kiki do everything together, and she's the type of person to call her dog her child. But Liz repeats herself, and it sounds exactly the same the second time. I shake my head. "What do you mean? Why would Mila give you Kiki?"

"She didn't give me many details, but it sounds like Aero thinks Kiki attacked another dog, so he's saying he won't report the bite if she gets rid of Kiki." Liz shakes her head as she speaks. Clearly, she already knows how ridiculous it sounds.

"But Kiki obviously didn't bite another dog, right? Unless she had a good reason," Like if Kiki bit Aero for being mean to Mila, I'd totally understand.

"Yeah, Mila says it was all a misunderstanding. Their neighbor made it up apparently."

I roll my eyes. "Let me guess, that lady had a Doodle that wasn't trained but she still thinks the calm neighbor dog is the problem because she 'looks scarier.'"

To my surprise, Liz chuckles, but then she quickly stops when she realizes I'm serious. "Sorry, but you sound exactly like Mila. You're probably right, but it's funny because I don't know anyone else who goes on animal welfare rants as much as my sister."

In any other circumstance, I might find Mila and I's similarities amusing, but this is a really serious situation. "Are you going to take Kiki then?"

"Well, I have no interest in owning a dog, especially since I have very little free time between work and school. But I can't let Kiki go to a stranger or the shelter. Plus, I've lived with her for several years, so I know how to care for her," Liz says. "However, I don't understand why she can't just break up with him and leave with Kiki. If anything would be a deal-breaker for Mila, this would be it."

I nod. "Yeah, I agree, but I think I can understand why. From this point on, if she does anything to upset

Aero, he might threaten to report Kiki's so-called attack. With the neighbor as a 'witness,' there's a chance Kiki will be put down because of her breed. I definitely believe Mila would put her own safety in jeopardy to save Kiki's life."

"Oh my god. I didn't think of it like that."

"Is there anything we can do?"

Liz thinks for a moment. "Well, she's dropping off Kiki tomorrow morning. If Aero's coming along, I might have a plan. But I'd like you to be there, if you can."

I smile. "Of course. I'll do whatever I can to save Mila and Kiki."

Chapter Twenty-Six
Mila

Kiki bounces with excitement as we near my old apartment. It still feels weird calling it that. Even though I've lived an entirely different life these past few weeks, this place is still home to me. Kiki pulls toward the door, not realizing that this moment will change both of our lives immensely. I'm not ready for it.

I glance back at Aero, who's yanking Kiki's crate out of the car. It's unfolded and filled with most of her supplies. She's crate trained, but I never make her go inside unless a maintenance person stops by. Otherwise, it's just a safe space if she wants to relax in it.

Aero kept suggesting we make her sleep in her crate, but I was able to convince him to at least let her sleep in a dog bed in our room. Before I moved in with Aero, she always slept in my bed, snuggled up against me.

Aero struggles to lift the full crate, but I know he won't feel "manly enough" if I help him. So, instead, I wait outside the front door with Kiki sitting next to me. Once Aero is beside me, he sets the crate down and glares at my innocent dog. "I can't wait for you and all your dog stuff to be out of my home."

Kiki tilts her head, not understanding what he's saying, but I can hear him perfectly. As if this whole situation wasn't bad enough, that statement makes my blood boil. Not only does he prefer to send my best friend away from me, but he's looking forward to it. He doesn't seem to feel an ounce of regret.

"Mila, what are you waiting for?" he asks after a few moments of silence. "Ring the doorbell."

I never thought I would be so unwilling to do something my soulmate asks, but the way he demands it gives me a huge ick. Was all this dreaming about a soulmate a waste of time? Did I let romance movies blind me too much?

I take a deep breath and ring the doorbell. In only a few seconds, Liz appears from behind the door. Her face lights up when she sees me, and to my surprise, her smile doesn't falter when she notices Aero behind me. "Come on in."

As we step inside, I let Kiki off her leash. She runs straight to Liz and wags her tail so fast her butt wiggles. Kiki and I have met up with Liz a few times since the move, but it's nothing compared to seeing her at home every day.

Then, after cuddling up next to my sister for a few moments, Kiki moves her attention to the other side of the room. She rushes over to the kitchen table with her whole body wiggling. My jaw drops when I see who's sitting there.

"Rory! What are you doing here?" I ask. I want to run up and give her a hug, but I'm sure Rory and Aero would both be a little uncomfortable with that.

Rory glances at Liz for a moment and then smiles. "Well, I've been hanging out with Liz a little bit lately, and she said I should stop by. She thought Kiki would be more comfortable adjusting to a home without you if she had more than one familiar face around."

I want to cry, but I don't know if the tears are happy or sad. Happy because Liz and Rory are so thoughtful and will take great care of Kiki. But sad because it's hitting me that I'm saying goodbye to my dog. Sure, I'll still see her when I visit Liz, but that's not enough.

"Mila, I don't like that your ex is here. Can she go to another room until we leave?" Aero scoffs.

I look at him and frown. "For the last time, she's not my ex. She's my friend. And you heard her, Liz invited her, not me. My sister has every right to invite whoever she wants into *her* apartment."

I cannot believe I just talked to him like that! As soon as it's out of my mouth, my eyes widen in terror. I see him looking down at me like I'm a fly he wants to flick away. He leans close to me. "We'll talk about your attitude later," he whispers into my ear.

I glance at Liz out of the corner of my eye, wondering if she heard that interaction. She looks worried, but she keeps a smile plastered on her face.

Aero clears his throat once he has stepped away from me. "A few more of Kiki's supplies are still in the car. Babe, would you help me grab them?"

I'd once dreamed of someone calling me Babe. Now, it sounds unsettling, as if it's an insult. I nod cautiously and follow Aero out to the car. It's clear that he doesn't trust me to be away from him. Not that I'd do anything, though. If I upset him too much, Kiki could be a goner.

I follow him out to the car and he opens the trunk. As I reach for a bag full of dog supplies, he sighs heavily, and before I know it, he's yelling.

"How dare you talk to me like that in there? Especially in front of your sister and former lover! Lately, you've been acting like I'm the bad guy, but I'm just trying to do what's best for us and our relationship. So, I hope you're done making me look like a fool."

Part of me wants to scream back at him. I want to remind him that Rory was never my "lover" and if he doesn't want to be treated like the bad guy, then he should stop acting like one.

But I can't say the things I want to say. I've accepted that now. If I want to keep him happy and Kiki safe, then I need to try harder to be what he considers a good girlfriend. I lower my head and nod before taking the bag back toward the house. That simple response seems to satisfy him enough because he smirks and picks up the other remaining pet products before following me back into the apartment.

When we re-enter the apartment, Liz and Rory are both sitting at the kitchen table with Kiki beside them. They freeze and turn toward us as we enter, as if we're interrupting an important conversation. I know they were probably gossiping about my relationship with Aero.

"Oh, look, I think your sister is falling in love with your old fling," Aero chuckles as he enters. I clench my fists. All I can think is, 'what the hell is wrong with him?' But I force myself to relax.

Luckily, Kiki rushes over to me and showers me with kisses to help me calm down. When I look up at Liz and Rory, I see them both glaring at Aero out of the corner of their eyes. I knew they weren't his biggest fans before, but I'm sure today's interactions made them hate him even more. I totally understand why.

Liz stands up and crosses her arms. "So, Aero, would you mind explaining exactly what happened with Kiki and the neighbor the other day? Mila didn't give me a lot of details over the phone."

She probably expects him to sweat a little, but he's confident. As long as he has at least one person to back up his claim that Kiki bit another dog, he has all the power.

He shrugs. "There's not much to tell. Mila was walking Kiki, and the neighbor claimed Kiki bit her dog. It's safer for everyone if Kiki stays out of that neighborhood."

"But you know Kiki didn't bite that dog, right? Kiki wouldn't hurt a fly."

"Does it matter if she did it or not? She's a Pit Bull. We don't need that kind of dog around our nice neighborhood."

I see Rory flinch at his words, and I know exactly how she feels. Ever since the situation with the Bernedoodle, Aero has stopped holding back his thoughts about Kiki. He's now the living embodiment of all the hateful Pittie comments I've seen on the internet. I wish I had been more skeptical of his feelings toward dogs when I met him. But now, it's too late.

"I'm sure Mila has told you that Pit Bulls aren't as dangerous as everyone makes them seem, right? As a dog trainer, she should know dog behavior better than the average person," Liz says. I'm not sure why she's trying to get him riled up. Isn't she worried he'll stop me from being around her too?

"I'm not saying whether Mila is right or wrong. I'm just saying that our neighbors dislike Pit Bulls, so it's best to keep that dog away from them."

"So, you never saw Kiki attack?"

"What is this, an interrogation? Are you a cop? No, I wasn't there, but the neighbor lady was screaming and saying that Kiki attacked."

"And you believe her over your own soulmate? That's messed up."

Aero glares at me. "Mila, I didn't realize your sister was so rude."

"Rude?" Rory speaks up. "How is she rude? Liz is taking on a huge responsibility of caring for a dog because of you. The least you could do is provide a little more context. If she's being given a dog with a bite record, she deserves to know." Her face is bright red and I notice her arms shaking as she speaks.

Aero locks eye contact with Rory for a few moments, then he glances back at Liz. "Fine. No, I did not see Kiki bite the other dog. I have never seen her act aggressive. You're not getting a dog with a bite record, which means you have no reason to change your mind about taking her." He takes a deep breath. "But you are still getting a Pit Bull, so I'd be cautious if I were you."

Part of me wishes Liz or Rory would punch him in the face. Is it horrible that I'd wish that for my partner?

But instead of exploding with anger, both Liz and Rory relax a bit. In fact, I swear I see Liz smirk. "Thanks, that's all I wanted to hear," she says calmly.

After a few moments of awkward silence, Aero puts his hand on my shoulder and sighs. "Alright, Mila, hurry up and say goodbye to your dog so we can get out of here. We have some errands we need to run."

'Saying goodbye to my dog' sounds way too harsh. It makes it seem like this is the end. As if I'll never see her again. In a way, I suppose that's accurate. I'll get to see her whenever I visit my sister, but I won't get to cuddle with her at night or go for long walks with her anymore. I won't get to do all the things I've done every day since I adopted her. And for that reason, my eyes well up with tears.

Before I can stop myself, I'm crying with Kiki in my arms. I hug her tightly, hoping that somehow my love for her can keep us together. She gives me a few slobbery kisses, which only makes me cry harder.

I feel someone else join the hug, and I look up to see Liz crouched down with her arm around me. Despite the tears streaming down my face, she's smiling. How can she be smiling at a time like this?

"Mila, please stop crying. You don't have to leave Kiki," she says.

"Huh?"

"You don't have to say goodbye to Kiki. Stay here. Move back in."

Before I can react, Aero butts in. "She's not moving back here. She lives with me."

Liz stands up to face him as she crosses her arms. "Is that because she wants to stay? Or because you're threatening to report her dog?"

"She wants to stay, of course. I'm the love of her life."

"So, if I had evidence of you admitting the dog bite was fake, she'd still want to live with you? Even though there's no threat of you reporting Kiki anymore?"

"What evidence?" He considers it for a moment, but I think I've put the pieces together before he can. I glance between Liz and Rory, and they're both smiling. They've set Aero up. All along they had a plan to keep me and Kiki together. How could I not have guessed it?

Liz points to the plant by the entryway. "Before you came over, Rory and I hid a camera in there. It recorded everything you just said about Kiki having no bite record." Before she even stops talking, he rushes toward the plant and pulls the camera out. "But I figured you'd try to destroy it or delete the footage somehow, so it's not the only one in the apartment. And Rory also recorded everything on her phone. So, even if one of the recordings isn't clear, we have backups."

He holds onto the camera tightly. I can see his face turning red, probably in a mix of anger and embarrassment. "Yeah, well, I can still report Kiki. Mila, come with me. We need to go."

Part of me wants to get up and obey him, but I don't move. I keep hugging my beloved dog. I glance up at Liz, waiting for her confirmation that Kiki is safe.

Liz winks at me. "Sure, Aero. If Mila stays here, you can still report Kiki's bite. But even though the government is often biased against certain dog breeds, they won't be able to argue with evidence. You'll just be wasting your time if you try it."

Honestly, I don't know if that's accurate or not, but Liz looks so confident as she speaks that I have no choice but to believe her. And clearly, Aero does too because his face goes from bright red to pale white. He's not used to losing.

He seems to be searching his brain for a good comeback or a way out of this situation, but when he comes up with nothing, he chucks the camera on the ground and breaks it. He clenches his fists and glares at me. "Come on, Mila. Let's go home. And since your sister is being ridiculous, you can bring your stupid dog back with us too."

And there it is. A chance to have both my soulmate and my dog in my life. It's what I've always dreamed of. But now, I finally understand that dreams aren't always what we expect them to be. Maybe it's better to wait for your dream to come true than to try to force it.

I stand up and look Aero in the eye. I mutter one simple but life-changing word: "No."

Chapter Twenty-Seven
Rory

"All your stuff has returned!" Liz announces as she sets a large box full of Mila's belongings on the ground. I follow behind her, setting a second large box onto the apartment floor.

It's surprising that Mila only had a few boxes of stuff at Aero's place. It's mostly just essentials, like clothes and toiletries. Either she knew deep down that she wouldn't be living there long or Aero didn't want her to bring all her dog-themed stuff. Now that I think about it, she brought the same amount of stuff for Kiki as she did for herself. It makes sense, considering how much Kiki means to her.

Mila rushes toward the entryway and wraps her arms around Liz. "Thank you so much! You two are life-savers." She lets go of her sister and glances at both of us with a huge smile. "I'm not even exaggerating. I thought I would be stuck with Aero forever. And the thought of returning to grab my stuff after that breakup was terrifying. I'm so grateful that you two were willing to get it for me."

"Of course, we were happy to do it," I say.

"Although, it was super awkward," Liz says. "Aero glared at us the whole time. And he kept saying you'd come running back to him in the future."

"Don't worry, Liz. I won't ever get back together with him. Even if he changes his entire personality," Mila says. "I've finally realized that being single isn't the worst thing in the world. But settling for someone like him is one of them."

"Finally, you're listening to my advice," Liz says. She pauses for a moment. "I'm grateful that Sawyer was nowhere near as bad as Aero. At least Sawyer is more likely to improve himself and find a compatible partner, I believe."

Mila nods. "Yeah, Aero will never be part of a healthy relationship until he can accept that he isn't perfect." She crouches down and looks through her boxes. "I tried to report him to the SoulSearcher Help Center, but they said since he hasn't done anything illegal, they have no reason to suspend his account from the online platform."

"Wow," I say. "I hope he doesn't prey on another hopeless romantic."

Mila nods, and I see her eyes water slightly, but she blinks the potential tears away. "Me neither, but sadly, there will always be people out there that behave like him. So, I've decided that I'd like to start some sort of support group for survivors of abusive relationships." She turns to me. "I know you've benefited from talking to people who understand you, so maybe I will too. And maybe I can help others in the process."

"That's a wonderful idea," I say. "I bet Zaya could help you set something like that up, if you'd like."

Mila smiles. "I'd like that a lot. I'd love to get to know her." Then, she glances at Liz, who's casually listening to our conversation. "Liz, I don't mean to be rude, but would you mind if I talk to Rory alone for a little bit? I haven't gotten a chance to since I left Aero."

"No worries," Liz says. "I'm sure you have lots to catch up on." She disappears into her room and closes the door behind her. I glance around awkwardly, not sure what Mila wants to tell me that she can't say in front of her sister.

Mila walks over to the kitchen table and sits down. Kiki rushes over to her and licks her leg, even though Mila has been home the whole time. Mila motions for me to sit on the opposite side from her, so I do. She stares into my eyes for a few moments, which is normally something I'd be uncomfortable with, but I'm just so happy to have her back that I don't really mind.

"Do you still have your SoulSearcher?" she asks.

My stomach sinks. Of all the things I thought she would say to me, I didn't think it would be that. "Um, yes. It's in my purse."

"Could you please put it on?"

"Mila, I'm not going down that road again. Just because—"

"Calm down, Rory," she interrupts. "I'm not hitting on you or longing to be with you. I'm just curious about something."

"Okay," I say hesitantly. Since I have no good reason to decline, I reach into my purse. I feel around until I find the small, zippered pocket that I store my SoulSearcher in. I gently pull out the bracelet and admire it for a few moments. It really is a nice piece of jewelry. Too bad wearing it makes everyone assume you're looking for love.

I put the bracelet on my wrist for the first time since it lit up for Mila. I look across the table at her, and something illuminates beneath me again. I glance down at the circular pendant, which is glowing without a doubt.

"Wow," Mila says before I can remind her that it's not what it seems. "You were right."

"I was?"

She nods. "Yeah, I think our SoulSearchers lit up for each other because we were meant to be in each other's lives, but not necessarily in a romantic way. I think we're supposed to be friends. We have a lot of the same values, and I always feel comfortable around you. I hope you feel the same about me."

"Of course."

"Anyway, I know I don't have my SoulSearcher anymore, but I guarantee it would still light up in return," she says. "I just want to make sure you know how sorry I am for my past behavior. I wanted to be in a relationship so badly that I risked losing an important friendship."

"I forgive you." I reach out and take her hand. Then, I smirk. "You were pretty crazy before though."

She giggles. "Yeah, that's true. And don't get me wrong, I still really want to fall in love and all that, but I want to make sure it's right before I start a serious relationship with someone."

The moment seems over, so I pull my hand away. "Will you get your SoulSearcher back?"

She shakes her head. "No, I don't really like the idea of a SoulSearcher anymore. I'm glad it works for some people, but now, I see that it goes wrong more often than people think. I'm planning to keep searching the old-fashioned way so I can choose who my perfect match is. And this time, I'll make sure it's someone who would never put my dog's life at risk."

"Yeah, that seems like the bare minimum for a partner."

She grins. "Yep, I realize that now. If any of the people I date have big red flags, you better be honest with me, even if I'm in love."

"Oh, I will. Even though that didn't go so well last time."

"I promise I'm going to try to be less blinded by 'love' from now on. Hopefully, that'll give me more common sense."

I smile but hesitate for a few moments before I get out the words I want to say. "Just so you know, I'm planning to turn in my SoulSearcher. I don't want to get matched with someone else and end up confusing them too. Is that okay?"

For a second, Mila's eyes look like they're about to release a puddle of tears, but she smiles back. "Yeah, I get it. I know it's what you should've done in the first place, but part of me is glad you didn't. Who knows if we would've met otherwise."

Now, my eyes feel like they're watering. "Okay, that's enough emotional talk for now. I need to tell you all about Tyson's adoption!"

"Awe, Tyson got adopted?"

"Yeah, shortly after the Pride event. His adopters were so patient. They met with him several times to gain his trust before adopting him."

We talk and laugh together for a while longer, and it feels like we've been this close forever. As we continue to discuss life, I can't stop feeling overjoyed that my best friend is back.

Chapter Twenty-Eight
Mila

I rush to the smoothie shop with Kiki's leash in one hand and a bouquet of flowers in the other. Kiki has no problem keeping up with me. Her adorable ears flop with every leap and bound. I stop at a table right outside my destination, and Kiki's tail won't stop wagging.

"Sorry, I'm late! My date went a little longer than I expected," I say.

My friends all look up at me and smile. Rory is there with Minnie in her lap and Liz is sitting next to her, petting Rory's latest foster dog, a white dog with brown spots named Jordan. Across from them are Zaya and Elijah, two of Rory's friends who I've grown close to these past few months. Elijah's Golden Retriever named Daisy appears from underneath the table to give Kiki a kiss, and Jordan tries to sniff her, but his leash won't reach that far. Kiki wags her tail like crazy and spins in circles so quickly that I almost trip over her leash.

"You need to give us all the details!" Zaya says as I attempt to untangle Kiki's leash from my leg.

I sit down at the only empty seat left. There's already a strawberry smoothie sitting there. I look at Rory and smile. Of course, she knows my usual. I wouldn't expect anything less.

I set the flowers down next to my drink. "As you can probably see, I got flowers. Which is nice, but I'm not letting it influence my feelings. The date was fun, but I don't know if I feel a spark yet. I'll give it another date or two to see if any connection builds." I take a sip of my drink. "I've been upfront with him the whole time about my feelings, and he has done the same. So, I really appreciate how patient and understanding he is."

"Wow, that sounds like the most mature date I've ever heard." Liz giggles. "Which is a good thing."

"Yeah, and of all the dates you've been on, this is the happiest I've seen you after one," Rory adds.

She's right. I've been on a lot of mediocre dates since parting ways with Aero, and I've rarely gone on a second date with someone. After ignoring so many of Aero's red flags, I can't afford to miss any incompatibility issues early on. No matter how much I like someone, I'm no longer afraid to tell them no if something feels off.

But this last date was great. It didn't feel like something out of a fairy tale book or anything, but I'm beginning to realize that isn't how the most successful relationships start. Instead of butterflies in your stomach and being swept off your feet, comfort and honesty are where it's at.

"It was definitely one of the better dates I've been on. But, of course, it helped that Kiki got to tag along."

"And how did he like Kiki?" Rory asks as she leans forward. This is always the biggest question for her, as it should be. After all, if you date me, you're going to be around my dog a lot too.

"He loved her," I say. "In fact, he seemed to like her more than he liked me. Which honestly, isn't a bad thing."

Everyone laughs, then goes back to sipping their drinks. Rory clears her throat and glances around nervously. "I just wanted to let everyone know that things are going well with my mom."

"Really?" I say with a smile.

She nods. "Yeah, she seems to have finally accepted that I'm never going to date anyone. I know it's still confusing for her, but I'm happy that I can finally be honest about everything with her."

"That's awesome, Rory," Zaya chimes in before I can say the same thing.

Rory nods, but her face turns red when she realizes she has caused an awkward silence. Luckily, Zaya is quick to change the topic to something she's working on at the LGBTQ+ Center. Everyone engages in the conversation with big smiles.

These little hangouts only started recently, but I look forward to them more and more each week. Friends like these are what I need in my life, and I can't believe I waited so long to find them.

Sure, I still want to find love like I always have, but I don't feel desperate or empty like I used to without it. I've learned that friendships can be just as important as significant others, and even when you're in a relationship, you still need to hold those friends close.

One day, I'll find my soulmate, but I'm in no rush. Instead, I'll just keep enjoying time with the other important people in my life while I keep looking for true love.

Acknowledgements

The idea of necklaces leading you to your soulmate has been an idea in my head for a long time. I first thought of it back in high school, and in college, I used the concept for a story bible assignment. Back then, it was just an ordinary romance story, but I received a lot of great feedback from classmates and teachers, which I'm very grateful for.

For years after that, I used a similar concept for many short stories, including one where a woman named Rory mistakenly got matched with a man even though she was gay. I thought all the idea would ever be is short stories like that, but when I was trying to create a story that involved asexual and bisexual characters, my mind wandered back to this premise. It became a new story with new characters, and I feel like I really made it into something special.

I want to extend a huge thank you to two people who helped me get this book to exist: Lacey Verrill and Grace Zimmermann. Lacey did an incredible job editing the book, just like she did with my first book, Save Our Dogs. Grace designed the cover, and she helped my vision for the cover come to life perfectly. It's exactly what I hoped for, and I can't stop looking at it because I love it so much.

I also want to say a general thank you to all the important people in my life, both friends and family. Everyone was so supportive with the release of my first book, and they've continued to support me as I worked on this book. When I first decided that this was a book I wanted to publish, I was really nervous because LGBTQ+ books aren't well-received by everyone. But luckily, I'm surrounded by so many loving, positive people, and that's what ultimately made me confident enough to finish SoulSearcher and publish it.

Thank you to everyone who read this book. I really hope you enjoyed it, and I hope the LGBTQ+ representation helps readers feel seen. If you liked it, please consider leaving a review on Goodreads, Amazon, and anywhere else you review books. It makes a huge difference for indie authors like me!

Molly Weinfurter is a writer who specializes in animal content. She has a Bachelor of Fine Arts in Creative Writing, and she has a sweet little rescue dog named Mabel. She loves doing what she can to help dogs in need, including fostering, volunteering at rescue events, and educating about puppy mills. To encourage more people to adopt dogs, she made sure the main characters in *SoulSearcher* have a strong passion for animal rescue too.

Check out Save Our Dogs by Molly Weinfurter!

Like most kids, Paisley has always dreamed of getting a dog. But when she's finally given a beautiful Dalmatian puppy for her 12th birthday, she also learns that her parents have been running a secret dog breeding business for years.

The dogs are kept in an old barn 24/7, and while it seems odd to Paisley, she trusts that her parents know what they're doing. She's eager to help her mom and dad care for the breeding dogs at first, but over time, she suspects that her parents might not be treating the dogs well.

Once Paisley learns that her parents' business is really a puppy mill, she only has one thing on her mind: saving the dogs.